Ricky Marcel's been in LA for eleven months, struggling to prove his dad back home in Bourbon, Kansas, wrong. Very wrong. Ricky has the chops to make it as an actor. He proves it every day, charming not only his customers at the restaurant where he works, but also the numerous casting agents he sees for auditions.

When he's called in to read for a super-secret series, Ricky's stunned to find he's on the fast track to a fake reality show about gay gigolos. He's been in the closet so long he has no clue where the key is located. But the fancy Bel Air pad that comes with his job, not to mention the money, influence him to go for it.

Then there's Drake Hardy, a mysterious figure who is not only incredibly sexy, but the show's producer. The attraction between the two men is immediate. Yet Ricky becomes frightened when he learns that Drake is a Dom. Can Ricky not only be a whore on TV, but Drake's personal sex slave as well?

This book is a work of fiction. Names, characters, places, and incidents either are products of the author's imagination or are used fictitiously. Any resemblance to actual events or locales or persons, living or dead, is entirely coincidental.

Just a Gigolo
Copyright © 2019 A.J. Llewellyn
ISBN: 978-1-4874-2446-6
Cover art by Martine Jardin

Published by eXtasy Books Inc or
Devine Destinies, an imprint of eXtasy Books Inc

Look for us online at:
www.eXtasybooks.com or www.devinedestinies.com

Just a Gigolo
Bought and Sold

By

A.J. Llewellyn

DEDICATION

To Adam Killian – still my muse.

CHAPTER ONE

Ricky Marcel sat in the outer office of Jessica Bentley & Associates Casting and studied the 'sides' that the assistant had given him. He had to learn these lines, even though they made no sense because he had no idea what they related to. He sighed. Nobody had told him about this aspect of auditioning in Hollywood. In an effort to preserve some mystery on top secret productions, actors weren't given any information. No title, no producer's name, no director, no character breakdown.

Just lines of dialogue he had to memorize.

Oh, and his agent's direction to dress 'upscale, but hot.'

He could not screw up this audition any more than he already had. He'd blundered badly with the annoyed-looking man sitting at the desk by trying to shake hands with him.

"We don't do that," Peter Duchesne had said in a nasty tone, checking Ricky's name off his call list with a forceful tick. Ricky had been taken aback. He'd noticed the sign on the wall too late. His gaze flew once more to the huge black and white notice that read: *Due to too many dirty hands and too many colds caught by our office staff, we will no longer be shaking hands. Thank you.*

Ricky still couldn't get over those words.

Toto, we sure ain't in Kansas anymore. He thumbed the silver dog key ring in his pocket. His pa had given it to him. Ricky had been stricken, hoping for cash, when he hopped the Greyhound from Bourbon County, Kansas, to Los Angeles. Pa had been trying to let Ricky know that in spite of his disapproval of his career plans, Ricky was welcome back home any time he wanted. The keys had become a good luck symbol to him, even if they were currently useless.

Eleven months later, the silver key ring with his family's house keys made him feel better on his bad days. And sometimes they were very bad. In fact, everyone in LA told him the first year here was the toughest. He had to give himself props for sticking it out. His fingers curled around the metallic dog's ears. He felt like Dorothy, except somebody had forgotten to give him a pair of ruby shoes and he'd yet to meet the wizard.

He swallowed over the lump in his throat. It was hard lying to Pa. But lately things *were* sort of looking up. He'd graduated from bad days to bad *hours*. Sometimes, like now, there were bad moments. He'd recovered from his hand-shaking gaff, accepted the sides and taken a seat. To his dismay, once again, as always at these casting calls, a roomful of hopefuls surrounded him. They all looked similar to him. Handsome, dark-haired guys with brown eyes and muscular builds. Ricky's hair needed a cut. It grew curly as it got longer. He would have gone to the barber before the audition, except he'd only been given an hour's notice to be here. He glanced around at the others.

They'd all apparently been given the same instructions and wore dress pants and shirts, except for one off-beat looking guy who wore leather pants, an ill-fitting leather vest and had his nose, eyes, lips and ears all pierced. He surreptitiously rubbed at his crotch, trying to shield his actions with his script sides. Probably his cock was pierced, too. Ricky took a second look at him. He was certain Mr. Leather was a recently retired gay porn star. If so, he had the condom-full-of-walnut look down pat.

What's his name? I know I've seen him in some Falcon Studios movies . . .

Ricky took a deep breath and his glance fell on the sign

2

once more. He'd never seen one like it before and decided it was rude. He tried to imagine anyone back in Kansas propping up a sign like that and he couldn't. He just couldn't.

The door to the inner sanctum swung open and each and every actor froze. Some had been mouthing the dialogue to themselves, others just reading.

"Jasper Jericho?" A young female associate stood in the doorway, staring across the top of all the dark heads in the office, looking for him. It was Mr. Leather. If he was the gay porn star, his real name was sillier than his fake one. Mr. Leather stood, a menacing air enveloping him as he followed the girl at the door.

Ricky and the others relaxed. He'd been on a trillion auditions like this one. He tried to look on the positive side. Ever since he'd been picked up by theatrical agent Stephen Granger three months ago, he'd been fortunate enough to land a ton of casting calls. His two roommates, Max and Colin, said some actors were lucky to go out on as many calls in a whole year.

Ricky was just grateful he'd been in a good mood the day he'd waited on Stephen Ranger in his day job as a waiter at Jerry's Famous Deli. Everybody said Jerry's had the name famous in the middle of it because most of the wait staff went on to great careers. He was beginning to despair that it was wishful thinking. He still worked there, but Stephen was positive the moment they started talking that he could get Ricky work.

That had been a good moment. A bad one followed quickly, when Stephen asked, "Are you gay or straight?" As Ricky hesitated, Stephen said, "You're gay, right? Doesn't matter. Just don't tell anybody."

Ricky had no intention of telling anybody. He'd kept his secret his entire twenty-six years in Bourbon County. He wasn't about to start blabbing now. He thought about Shellene, the girl he'd dated as a kind of beard. She'd wept when Ricky wouldn't bed her. They all thought he was a religious fanatic back home. He'd had to think of something when Shellene involved the entire town in their sex crisis.

And now he was in Hollywood, trying to convince Pa he'd made it. He hadn't mentioned that the guy who owned the house he and two other guys were renting had failed to pay his mortgage for over a year and the bank had foreclosed. Ricky and his roommates would need to move, but nobody would tell them how long they had. Stephen had told him the bank would give them plenty of notice.

Deep breath, deep breath. That's right. You can't go in there stressed.

"What about Shellene?" Pa had asked on the phone just an hour ago. "She's trying to hold on, son." Ricky had told her not to. He'd begged her to find somebody better. He and Pa had this conversation each time they talked.

As if I need to worry about her, too . . .

Ricky shook his head and looked at the lines on the page once more. Stupid lines. Dumb lines.

Who wrote this dreck, anyway?

Stephen had called him early in the morning telling him he was to audition for a top secret, 'scripted reality show.' That's what the industry now called alleged reality shows. He'd had no idea until he arrived in LA that most of these shows that had taken over television were scripted. He looked for a window, feeling a little claustrophobic. He never thought he'd miss wide, open spaces, but he did. More and more. The casting offices on Catalina Street in West Los Angeles alarmed him because everything was fake, even the plants.

"Ricky Marcel?" The female associate had returned. He held up his hand and stood, bumping a couple of ancient copies of Time magazine onto the floor. He bent and straightened them, plopping them on the coffee table again.

He caught the derisive expressions on a couple of the waiting actors' faces.

He recognized one of them as a valet driver for Jerry's and realized the old adage was true. Everybody in LA wanted to be in showbiz. Ricky followed the girl, who led him to a room where a gigantic woman with fire engine-red hair stood behind a camera barking at some poor flunky who cowered under her rage.

Ricky estimated she was at least six feet tall. Her hair was the color of a beetroot and her lipstick, nail polish and outfit matched. She looked like a gigantic, bleeding wound. She flicked a haughty glance at him mid-sentence and stopped speaking. In a matter of seconds, she'd sized him up and he'd taken the opportunity to look around the room. Completely empty except for several chairs and the camera with a tripod.

"Who's this?" the tall woman asked the girl who'd brought Ricky into the room. There was nothing on his resume except two plays and a TV commercial that hadn't aired, nor was it likely to, but he did have a copy of it, and he did have good photos though, thanks to Stephen's recommendation.

The tall woman groaned. "He's not even SAG ready," she mumbled, loud enough for them to hear her back in Bourbon. He said nothing. He already knew this. Being SAG ready meant that one had done enough work, usually five lines or more on a Screen Actors Guild-accredited TV show or movie. Being SAG ready meant that an actor was eligible to join the union but didn't have enough money to pay the hefty fees to join.

He'd learned not to argue with casting people. He now had to remember not to touch them, either. The woman kept muttering under her breath, but he stopped listening. He was trying to remember the bad dialogue. If he listened to any of her bitchy comments it would throw his performance.

She was looking at him through the camera now and Peter Duchesne entered the room, closing the door behind him. He gave Ricky a small smile. Ricky smiled back, receiving a whiff of something minty and melony fresh as Peter walked past him.

"Has anyone told you what we're casting today?" the tall woman asked.

He shook his head and she gave him a smug grin. "Ever heard of the reality show *Gigolos*?"

"No, I don't believe so." He racked his brain. He and his roomies had split a subscription for cable TV so that they would know all the hot shows. Gigolos had not been one any of them thought to watch.

Ugh. I'm about to strike out again.

"We're casting the gay version of it," the tall woman said. She watched him for a reaction and she got it. His face flamed and he wanted was to sink through the floor.

She knows I'm gay! Stephen told her! He told me not to tell anybody! I wanna kill myself! No. I'll kill him first, then knock myself off . . .

"We're going to set up five gay gigolos in various luxury homes around town." She pointed to a blue folder he'd never seen before. He picked it up and leafed through the scant pages of high quality photos of five different mansions. He couldn't believe his eyes. The tall woman kept prattling as his hungry heart pined for the house he'd passed many times on Stradella, the ritziest street in LA.

"If you get the job, you'll move into one of these houses. Each one has five or six bedrooms. You'd be paid to pretend to be a gigolo. Some of your dates would involve nothing but talk, some might involve more. We're pretending these dates are real though, but you wouldn't be required to actually have sex."

He couldn't get over the gorgeous houses. The more she

talked, the more he liked the idea of becoming somebody else.

A character.

I'm an actor. I'm gonna get paid a boat load of money to pretend to be a whore.

He closed his eyes for one brief moment. It would be just like the Richard Gere movie, *American Gigolo*. He'd watched it on TV just the other night. The gigolo got to wear cool clothes, eat at the best restaurants. *Only I'd get to do it with hot guys. They'd have to be hot guys for TV. Not even the extras are ugly in Hollywood.*

When he opened his eyes again, everybody was smiling at him.

"Sounds good to me," he said. In spite of his fear of being outed, his panic over what Pa would say, he wanted this. Pa didn't have cable TV anyway. He'd make up a fake name and not tell anyone he knew that he was doing the show. He forgot about everything else but all the good things he could do with his money. He allowed his gaze to caress the camera. He'd become quite adept at all kinds of auditions. Cold readings still frightened him, but the prospect of actual work, of money, *real* money and no longer having to ask, "You want fries with that?" coaxed the best line delivery he'd ever given.

Peter Duchesne solved the mystery of the lines in between those Ricky had on his sides. They ran through the scene once. Ricky was embarrassed when Peter asked if Ricky would really be willing to do anything for the client. Ricky assured him he would. After one go through, they did it for the camera. Their banter was even better the second time and Ricky had to squash down the idea that he was flirting with a handsome guy in front of total strangers.

They shot the scene a second time, from a different angle. The dialogue wasn't so bad now. Ricky somehow made it seem sexy and original when he promised the camera,

"Whatever you want me to do, I'll do. I'm yours."

The tall woman and Peter both gave him two thumbs up.

"How would you feel about a cock cage?" the wall woman asked.

Ricky hesitated. Now, what in the world was a cock cage? Back home on the farm, they sometimes isolated cocks into wooden crates when they were about to be sold. Catching the damned birds was difficult, so he and Pa caught them when they could. Maybe there was a human equivalent. Some kind of kinky cage where the client of the gigolo kept him locked up until he was ready to play with him. It wasn't his kind of thing at all, but heck, as long as there was no pain involved, he could do it.

Aware of the intense gazes from the others in the room, he gave them a smile he hoped conveyed confidence and a little bit of lust.

"I'm fine with it," he lied. He'd never been near one in his life, but he was in character now and having the time of his life.

"So you'd be willing to wear one on camera?"

Wear what? What had he missed? Remembering everything he'd ever learned about being an actor, he kept his voice even. You had to lie, lie, lie. Like the time he said he could ride horses but had never been on one in his life.

He gave the tall woman a lopsided grin. "Now?" he asked.

"No, eager beaver." She actually laughed. "I'll be in touch." As he thanked the three other people in the room and turned on his heel to leave, he felt funny not shaking hands with any of them. He must have done well though, because the tall woman whispered dramatically, "He's a sexy thing, isn't he?"

It was only when he was halfway home in his banged up 1997 Ford Taurus that reality hit him. Nobody had introduced him to the tall woman, and the idea of a chastity belt petrified him.

He was delighted to find parking right outside the tiny house he shared with Max and Colin on Orlando Avenue. Bang-slap in the heart of the sprawling mass of what the post office called Los Angeles, and residents insisted Beverly Hills Adjacent, he loved the place. Ricky checked the front door as he parked the car. No nasty eviction notice. Thank God. He ran inside. Max and Colin were a couple but pretended they weren't. Max was also an actor, and Colin was a tennis pro. He'd been the one who secured the lease on the house with his endorsement money. He and Max had fallen in love a few years before and Max moved in with him.

Tennis pros were a bit like actors. They could make great money when they worked, but they suffered harsh professional winters. A torn tendon had sidelined Colin — for now.

Ricky had met Max at work and hit it off immediately. Four weeks later, he gave up his roach-infested apartment in Koreatown and moved in with Max and Colin. It had been great. Over the last few years, they told him, none of their roommates had any sense of responsibility. Ricky had been a godsend.

Everything would have been peachy, had the foreclosure not been looming over their heads. Their landlord had neglected to pay the mortgage for months and they lived month to month, paying rent money into an escrow account. The bank had advised them to do this. The landlord was pissed. It was a bit like living in Beirut, except everybody dressed better.

Ricky's cell phone rang just as Max poked his head out of the kitchen door and asked, "How'd the audition go?"

"Great!" Ricky checked the cell phone's ID screen. It was Stephen.

"They loved you," his agent burbled the moment Ricky

took the call. "I have it on good authority that they loved your whole shy, but sexy country boy routine. I know you've been taking voice classes to lose your twang, but you must stop them immediately. They want you twangin' away." A pause. "They also want you to attend a cocktail party tonight to meet the other short-listed guys."

Ricky began to sway. How would he get through something like that?

"I'd go with you, but nobody else is taking their agent," Stephen said, correctly reading Ricky's expressive silence.

"How do you know that?" Ricky asked.

"Well, two of the other actors are my clients. One of them is the ex-porn star Ace Andrews. That's why it would be impossible for me to split my affections, but I'm rooting for ya, kid."

Ricky lapsed into a stunned silence. Was it even ethical for Stephen to put up multiple clients for the same gig?

"Why don't you take your cute roommates? They're a hoot." Stephen gave Ricky all the details and warned him to dress well for the event. "I heard one guy went all dressed in leather. They tell me he's on the short list. Hey gotta go. Have fun and I want a full report in the morning!"

Ricky ended the call and walked into the kitchen. The smell of sizzling *gyoza* on the stove made his mouth water. Max, who was Chinese and Hawaiian by birth, was a fantastic cook and whipped up homemade pot stickers and all kinds of yummy foods every day.

"Well!" He turned to smile at Ricky. "Tell me all about it."

Ricky did. He finished with, "And if I get the house, you and Colin have to move in with me."

"Oh!" Max raced over and hugged him. "You have such a beautiful soul. And integrity. You are so obviously not from around these parts, doll face!" He removed some *gyoza* from the frying pan, blotted them on a sheet of paper towels, then handed Ricky a few on a plate.

Ricky dipped one into Max's homemade teriyaki sauce.

"Enjoy those while you can," Max said.

"Why? Are you going to stop making them?"

"No, idiot. But once you're on TV, you can't eat things like this. When you're a gigolo you'll have to watch what you eat. It'll be lettuce sandwiches and mung bean soup for you."

Oh, no, it won't. Ricky loved his food. He and good eats would never, *ever* be parted.

"So eat up, big boy, then we need to pick out your wardrobe for this evening."

"I love you for this, Max."

Max gave him a huge grin. "I'm not doing it for you, sunshine. I'm doing it for the hot new house we might all get."

Ricky had never been so nervous in his life. Showing up at the swanky house in the Hollywood Hills was frightening enough. Especially with the snarled traffic snaking up Beachwood Canyon and its many, tiny streets jutting from it. Max drove, Colin in the passenger seat beside him trying to find a traffic station that would explain the snafu.

Sitting in back, Ricky could hear a coyote howling somewhere close and feared being eaten by one before he could get his chance at stardom. He tugged at his crotch.

"Stop it," Max said, glimpsing him through the rearview mirror.

A handful of valet drivers in red jackets ran down the hill and relieved each vehicle of its occupants.

"Ah," Colin said. "This must be some big shindig! They've hired professional parking."

Ricky observed an irate resident shouting at a hapless valet driver who was just trying to do his job.

"The neighbors are hatin'." Max grinned as he handed his

BMW to a valet who didn't look old enough to drive. They watched him zoom off with a screech of brakes.

"Oh, dear." Max looked a bit horrified.

"We're insured," the ever-practical Colin reminded him.

When Ricky thought his roommates were distracted, he surreptitiously tugged at the crotch of his tight pants.

Max slapped his hand away. "Stop picking your seat."

"I feel like a whore in this outfit," Ricky whispered as they trudged up the hill.

"You're supposed to look like a whore. You're a gigolo, baby!"

What on earth had possessed him to agree to wear a pair of Max's tightest black leather pants and to buy a white pirate shirt? *Pirate!* He'd give anything to be on the high seas . . . *anywhere* but here. He couldn't pull off being a gigolo. He should go home now, before he embarrassed himself completely. Sex to him was sacred. Sex was something he'd had with one man, and one man only, Jimmy Lewis, who'd left him after a bad argument, gone off to the mall in Kansas City and got his ass signed up to the Marines.

Jimmy had died in Iraq, his entire squadron killed in a tank explosion.

Don't think about that. He's dead. He can't see you on TV.

Ricky began to really worry now. It had been hard enough undressing in front of the man he'd loved, let alone on . . . camera.

A few houses down from the one with all the lights, cameras and security personnel milling about, Max fluffed Ricky's hair with expert fingers and gave him a once-over before allowing him to walk into the house.

"Your ass is divine, Ricky." He gave it a pat, making his boyfriend, Colin, laugh, but Ricky was mortified. He felt a hand shoving him forward and tripped on a ridiculous red carpet.

"Name?" a man in a black suit asked. He was wearing

sunglasses. At night. Ricky thought only Jack Nicholson and assholes did that. And this guy wasn't Jack Nicholson.

Ricky stumbled forward as cameras flashed and a voice boomed at him.

"Helloooo, darling!" It was the tall woman from his casting session. She wore a flowing emerald green dress and it shocked him to notice it was see-through. He could see all her parts and pieces. She threw herself at him and kissed his cheeks, though her mouth came close to his lips both times. He felt very uncomfortable when she seemed to rub her front up against his.

Somebody called over to her. "Jessica!"

This was the first time Ricky realized she was Jessica Bentley, the owner of the casting company. He kept the frozen smile on his face, though he inwardly cringed. He didn't want *any* part badly enough that he'd allow himself to be some kind of lunchmeat. She gripped his hand and tore off with him, plunging him into the crowd of handsome men. He spotted the retired gay porn star, who gave him a grin. He wore tattered jeans and a black silk shirt. He looked hotter than hell.

And I'm dressed like a pirate.

"Just the man I wanted to see," Jessica trilled, smiling hard at the gorgeous Amerasian man standing in front of them. He was so stunning, Ricky couldn't speak.

"Drake Hardy, meet Marcel."

"A pleasure to meet you." Drake took Ricky's hand.

Ricky started to sweat. He'd never been so close to anybody so beautiful and he knew his hand must be unpleasantly clammy in Drake's, but the other man was staring at him in a mesmerizing way. It made Ricky feel sexy and vulnerable all at the same time.

It had been on the tip of his tongue to correct Jessica by saying Marcel was his last name. Now he couldn't dig deep enough to find the resources to make even the smallest reply.

Eep, came to mind. A sudden flash entered Ricky's brain. He saw himself naked on his back on a rumpled bed, his hands and feet tethered to the bedposts.

He shook the image loose from his head and finally smiled. "The pleasure is all mine," he said with such sinful undercurrents he sensed the other man's surprise and delight even though his eyes gleamed only just a little. It was there in the extra pressure on Ricky's hand and the too-long gaze they mutually held.

When Drake finally released his hand, Ricky's whole body shook with a mixture of excitement and holy cow . . . *peril.*

As handsome as he was, Drake exuded a kind of danger Ricky had never experienced before. He was dressed in an expensive-looking charcoal suit with matching suede shoes and an open-necked black shirt.

Drake opened his mouth to say something to Ricky, but Jessica grabbed Drake's arm.

"There's somebody I want you to meet," she said loudly.

"To be continued," Drake murmured, catching Ricky's gaze before being hurtled away.

"Yeah. Oh, yeah," Ricky said, regretting his eager-puppy tone. He caught the amusement in Drake's eyes as Jessica steered him toward a group of elegant men laughing in earnest about something.

Sheesh. I sound so stupid. Are pirates supposed to be goofy?

"You have a new fan," said a voice in his ear. Colin.

Ricky couldn't help grinning at his roommate.

Max and Colin were the best. They were so supportive. He fretted when he thought about the three of them losing their lovely home. Max didn't want to be a waiter forever and he knew that things hadn't been so easy for his friends. He wanted them all to do well.

"You look stunning," Colin said. He was tall and blond, his eyes the color of butterscotch. A sharp contrast from his exotic-looking lover, but they were the happiest, rock-solid couple Ricky knew.

"Have you checked out the canapés?" Max asked, joining them as he stuffed his mouth with something that looked delicious. "Real crab meat. Not the fake stuff." Max held the stuffed crepe to Ricky's mouth. Ricky bit into it, hoping there was no garlic in it. He caught Drake's gaze just as he began to chew.

Oh, man, there isn't a person alive who looks sexy when they're eating, except the girls in those Carl's Junior commercials . . .

Ricky didn't want to smile, not with the creamy concoction in his mouth. And he didn't *not* want to smile. He settled for a small, clothed-mouth smile that apparently had an alarming effect because Colin suddenly said, "Are you in need of the Heimlich maneuver?"

The food would not go down. Ricky tried swallowing. The crab meat just rolled around in his mouth like a tennis ball. He was desperate to get rid of it, but couldn't. He cast around for a large potted plant or something he could spit it into, but there was nothing as far as he could see. He shook his head at Colin.

"Oh, look," Colin said. "There's a pool outside. Wait . . . is that Ace Andrews down there?

Ricky glanced outside the massive picture windows. It looked like an orgy was taking place in the pool. He was more impressed by the spectacular sight of chandelier lights dangling from trees around the pool.

"Ace Andrews?" Max craned his neck. "It *is* him. I'd recognize those cock and nipple piercings anywhere." They each gave Ricky a look.

"You mind if we go down to the pool?" Colin finally asked.

He waved them off, relieved he'd finished the rubbery

food.

"Disgusting wasn't it?" Max asked, grinning at him.

"Why did you let me eat it? It was horrible," Ricky gasped.

Max shrugged. "I thought it would be rude to leave it on a side table."

Ricky stared at him as he drifted off with Colin.

Now what to do?

He glanced around and noticed a couple of other nervous-looking guys and wondered if they were potential gigolos, too. He walked over to one guy, who ran off as though Ricky might bite him.

What's up with him?

Ricky felt hands gripping his shoulders and turned around to find the guy from the casting session earlier that day.

"Peter Duchesne," he said, extending his hand to him. Peter just stared at it. *Oh, yeah, right. He doesn't do that. What the fuck ever.*

A waiter swept past with an empty tray of champagne glasses. Ricky was starting to hate this whole party and wanted to leave.

I need fresh air, that's all.

He gave Peter a smile and said, "I'm going to get a drink," and walked off, hoping to find a kitchen or maybe a passing waiter with a full tray of drinks. He could get bombed and perhaps he could walk home. Screw the coyotes. Right now, he didn't care if they did attack him. This wasn't what he wanted for his big Hollywood career. He wandered down the brightly lit corridor to what looked like a separate, closed-off section. No kitchen in sight.

"Hi there."

Ricky almost jumped, surprised to find Drake stepping out of the shadows.

"Hi." Ricky's whole body vibrated with a strange quaking. He couldn't decide if it was good or bad.

"Having fun?" Drake asked.

"No." Ricky regretted his response immediately. He wondered how long he might last on skid row. He'd seen the latest TV reports. More and more Hollywood wannabe's were winding up on the worst street in downtown LA. It was his single, greatest fear in life; being homeless.

But Drake just laughed. "This isn't your usual thing?"

Ricky couldn't help smiling. The guy was really nice. "Naw. I like talking to people one-on-one."

"Me, too." Drake put his arm around Ricky's waist and led him into a dimly lit room.

It was clearly an office space, but the most well appointed one he'd ever seen. It was a mixture of luxury and high-tech, with leather sofas and reclines dotting the room, a massive flat screen TV against one wall and a bank of monitors along the other. A closer look revealed all the activity in every room of the house. Ricky could see a lot of cavorting in the pool on one screen, and yet more people trudging up the hill toward the house on another.

It looked like Ace Andrews was hiding in the bushes in a dark corner of the backyard giving head to two men whose cocks hung out of their pant flies. Ricky averted his gaze. He'd just recognized one of the men as Peter Duchesne. For some reason it disappointed him.

Ricky became aware of Drake's amused glance.

"What do you doing here?" Ricky asked. "Is this your house or are you head of security or something?"

"Kind of a mix of both. Actually, I own the house, and I'm the producer of the show. Since we'll be shooting it here, I've been involved with wiring the entire property with cameras."

"We're shooting the show here?" Ricky was dismayed. What about the fantastic houses he'd seen in the laminated pages of the folder during his casting session? A terrible second thought occurred to him. He'd spoken as if his participation was a done deal.

Shit.

"I mean, I didn't know you . . . everybody . . . um . . ." His voice fell away as he tried to recover from his gaffe.

"I like a confident man," Drake said, sending his gaze to the screen where Ace was blowing yet another guy in dark, secret places. Man, the guy was insatiable.

Drake gestured toward the screen. "This type of behavior is very off-putting to me. Don't let me catch you giving yourself away for free. On this show, I'll get you the most money you've probably ever seen in your life."

Ricky didn't know how to respond to this statement. It was as though Drake cared about him, yet, how could he? They didn't know about each other.

"Somebody once told me that actors should be whipped," Drake suddenly said. " But they should be whipped with lettuce leaves. What do you think of that statement?"

Ricky realized it was a test but he didn't think whipping anybody with lettuce leaves would do them any harm, though he knew a few guys in the kitchen at Jerry's Deli he wouldn't have minded flinging vegetables at.

"I'd say that lettuce leaves would be a tease."

Drake grinned and came over to him. The nearness of him sent Ricky's senses into a tailspin. Drake didn't touch him. He stood mere inches from him, their gazes holding. Ricky couldn't understand the pull he felt toward the man or why he had the sudden urge to throw himself on the ground and grovel at Drake's feet whispering, "Yes, master."

For a long moment, Ricky was certain Drake would kiss him, but he had the peculiar sensation the guy was drinking in his essence instead.

Drake leaned in so close, Ricky's body began to sway with

desire.

God help me. This guy's probably really bad news.

Drake spoke, his soft words drowning out the drums and cymbals crashing inside Ricky's addled mind. "I think we're going to get along just fine." His lips were so close, Ricky could almost taste them. He could almost taste the faint, delicious smell of Drake's skin. Drake put a finger to Ricky's lips as though to shush him.

He put his hands on Ricky's shoulders, spun him around and pushed him gently out of the office, closing the door behind him.

CHAPTER TWO

At eight o'clock the following morning, Ricky still had no idea if he was any closer to landing the part. He walked to work, gnawing over the embarrassingly long evening he'd endured. After leaving Drake's office, he'd stumbled around the house, finding himself being tossed into a room full of strangers. He and the other potential gigolos were asked lots of strange questions by men he'd never met and still had no clue who they were.

One odd-looking guy in a Sikh's turban asked him, "How old do you want to be when you die?"

The question had so freaked Ricky out that it took him a moment to respond. Wasn't this the sort of question a serial killer might ask his victim?

"I want to live a very long time," Ricky said. He stared at the turban, certain he saw something in it. "I think life is —"

The man had cut him off. "Is your family supportive of your being gay?"

"Absolutely not." Ricky didn't want to tell him the dreadful things Pa had done to him to stop him from being 'girly.' Pa had no idea he was gay.

Beside him, another prospective gigolo was saying, "My parents have been very supportive. My mom always says, 'I only tried to teach you to love. Who you love is bigger than a mom can teach.'"

Dang. That was some poetic stuff. Ricky had begun to fret that his one-word answers and general uneasiness would kill his chances. He did his best but he was out of his depth.

He walked into Jerry's Famous Deli, the familiar smell of baking bread and, tantalizingly, noodle kugel, he was certain he'd be here for the rest of his life. He greeted his shift manager, put on his black work apron and prepared to take his first breakfast orders of the day.

Oh, joy. The wannabe TV producer. Bob Cohen appeared to be happily married with two children, he operated out of a corner booth trying to put together a non-existent talk show, and he dipped his hook into the dating site Plenty of Fish, pretending he was single. His Facebook page listed his relationship status as 'It's Complicated' but when Bob came in with his family, it sure didn't look complicated. Ricky knew this because Bob had befriended him on the social networking site.

This morning Bob appeared to have set up a meeting with a man. That was a surprise. They were usually women. Ricky greeted them, offering them coffee and iced water. Bob was usually nice to Ricky, even if he was a dickhead. He'd sought Ricky's friendship and asked his last name. He usually left a twenty percent tip and always complimented Ricky's service. This morning, however, he was nasty.

He's trying to impress this guy. Doesn't he know it always pays to be nice to people who are handling your food? I could go spit in his poached egg if I wasn't a nice guy myself.

"Coffee for me." Bob stared at the man opposite him.

"Decaf," came the response.

"And make it snappy. I don't like my coffee cold," Bob said. Ricky kept a smile on his face. Being a waiter was the best experience an actor could have in shielding his emotions. He'd just seen Forest Whitaker's breathtaking turn as a White House butler in *Lee Daniels' The Butler* and still couldn't get over the actor's nuanced performance as a man forced to hide his feelings both at work and home. Whitaker's face resonated strongly in his mind. Even now he could feel the character's pain as he filled two cups and returned them to the table.

At Jerry's, the decaf coffee was poured into brown cups so the bus boys would know the difference.

"Mine's cold," Bob said, even as steam drifted upward from the rim.

Is he kidding me? Ricky kept his tone neutral and went and poured a fresh cup, even though there was nothing wrong with the first one. He had other things to worry about. What would he tell Stephen when they talked at ten o'clock?

It had been a disaster. A catastrophe. Though he felt a momentary stab of relief about not being a TV gigolo, he wanted to work. He wanted to be loved. He didn't want to pretend it didn't matter when customers were rude to you.

"I want a poached egg, medium, and don't overcook it this time. Yesterday I thought I was eating a tennis ball."

"No problem," Ricky said. He always took heat for the kitchen, but he knew there'd been nothing wrong with the egg.

"Would you like hash browns or cottage fries with that?"

Bob eyed him. "A side of cottage cheese."

Wow. He never ate cottage cheese. As he took the other man's order and went back and forth with their food, he began to realize Bob was lining up a threesome with the other man. What a creep. To Ricky's shock, as he returned to the table with their toasted bagels and topped up their coffees, he overheard Bob saying,

"My wife left it to me to organize this. We'll meet you at the hotel at five. I've arranged for a hooker to be there. I'm paying this chick by the hour. Don't be late."

Not a threesome, but a foursome. And holy cow. His gorgeous, sweet wife and a hooker!

It took everything in him to keep his face blank, to not tip the food and coffee all over Bob. He had to thank Forest Whitaker for that and realized just how hard it was to pull off such a feat.

Back in the kitchen, he pulled his cell phone from his pocket.

Stephen had left ten voice mail messages, and he'd texted him, too.

Ricky called him back, bracing himself for a barrage of verbal abuse.

"You're in," Stephen said. "Baby, you're fucking *in!*"

Ricky might have done the Snoopy dance all over the restaurant had he not heard the punch line. The evening had gone so well that eight actors had been selected, Ricky being one of them. Each of them were required that afternoon to record one-on-one interviews with the casting director. All the interviews would be forwarded to the studio, which, in this case, was Elysian Studios, which would broadcast the series on their new cable network.

Out of the eight interviews, five gigolos would be chosen. The name of the new series would be *Bought and Sold*. Oh, God, it sounded tacky, but work was work. And this one didn't come with fries and a side of bacon. He would no longer be going home smelling of cooking grease.

Elysian had been making a swift name for itself with high-budget movies and TV shows, most of them gay and lesbian oriented. *Bought and Sold* would be its first high-profile "reality" show.

"They're paying above union scale, way above it," Stephen said. He began tossing out numbers and mentioned free first class air travel, hotels, islands, mountains, Swiss chalets. "You'll live in a great house. I already told them you like the one on Stradella. But you'll get it for a guarantee of at least one year, whether the show flies or not."

Ricky couldn't take it all in. Even with Stephen's fifteen percent fee, he would be earning great money. He could finally save.

"I'm excited for you, honey." Stephen ended their conversation when Elysian called on the other line.

Ricky got through his shift, surprised that a flurry of negative reviews hadn't showed up on Yelp about his work that day. He was so busy planning what he'd wear and what he'd say in the interview that he kept mixing up his orders.

At three o'clock that afternoon he showed up at Jessica Bentley & Associates Casting. This time he was greeted like a family member. Nobody shook his hand but he got lots of smiles and several hugs. He'd been curious to see who the other gigolos were and wasn't surprised to see Ace Andrews there. He was a livewire, that one, and would undoubtedly have people tuning in to see what nonsense he got up to.

All eight actors were dressed in suits, as had been the directive. Ricky was wearing one of Max's Tom Ford suits. He'd paired it with a white shirt, black tie and shiny black shoes. He felt a bit like John Travolta in *Pulp Fiction* in it.

There was a blond guy with startling blue eyes that were almost purple. He looked cool in his shiny grey suit. Ace Andrews was wearing a cherry red suit that only he could have pulled off. His pale yellow snakeskin shirt and matching boots, he informed us, came from the hide of a twenty-foot albino anaconda.

I'll take his word for it.

Ricky glanced at the other guys. Not one was ugly, but obvious the casting people were looking for different shades of personality.

"Fuck, I think I'm having a heart attack," one of the guys said. "All that blow last night." He clutched his chest.

Ricky couldn't remember seeing any blow at the party house, but the guy seemed to be in deep distress.

"You need us to call 911?" he asked.

"No," the guy said. "I need this job." His face turned red, his body contorted. Ricky and Ace got to their feet, then suddenly the guy laughed. "Gotcha!"

"Asshole," Ace said.

Ricky concurred privately. He said nothing, and then the door swung open and Jessica caught his gaze.

"You're first up, Marcel."

He followed her into the room, Ace the only man wishing him good luck. He might have been a whore, but Ace seemed decent.

"Thanks," Ricky said, giving him a smile.

In the interview room, Peter Duchesne was the one conducting the questions. Some of them were easy. *Why did you come to Hollywood? Who's your favorite actor?* Then came, *What do you look for in a man?*

Ricky dragged up Forest Whitaker's face in his mind.

"Men who care about the people in their lives and will go to extraordinary lengths to give them what they need." Ricky was surprised by his own words. It sounded good.

"What about physical looks?" Peter asked.

"I'm not into looks as much as I am interested in a man's character." That part was true. "I like men. I find something attractive in all of them. But that's just me. I'm a country boy. We look for the good in everyone."

He started to laugh. He sounded so corny.

When the interview concluded he wasn't sure if he'd turned in the kind of responses they wanted. He went home and prepared himself for the long wait. He paced the house, not even Max able to make him stop worrying. Looking for work was one thing. Waiting to hear about an audition was another.

Getting to that next step was stress and pressure he hadn't expected. Actors didn't talk about the next step so much.

"That's because you might go through this a dozen times before you even get cast in something," Max told him when he mentioned it. "You start to realize it's the delicious part of auditioning, but it's still part of the process. There's an upside to it, though. Even if you don't get the part, word gets around that you went to studio."

To studio. Industry lingo, attached to me! Ricky tried to take heart in that.

He tried to take his mind off his cell phone not ringing by joining Colin and Max on a spirited two-mile walk around Silver Lake. They followed this up with dinner at Mandarette, their favorite Chinese cafe. They were halfway through a delicious meal of two of the house specialties—war soup and strawberry shrimp—when Ricky's cell phone rang.

It was Stephen.

Ricky was so distraught at the possibility of having screwed up the interview he couldn't take the call. Colin reached over and grabbed the cell phone.

"Hey, Stephen. It's Colin. What's the news?"

The sunburst smile on his face told Ricky everything he needed to know.

"You're in, baby!" Colin jumped up and hugged him. Ricky fought the urge to cry. This being a Hollywood restaurant, word scattered around the tables and everybody applauded. Ricky sniffed back the tears that threatened to fall.

He'd done it. He was on the inside.

Inside Hollywood.

CHAPTER THREE

Ricky quit his job the next day. He would finish out the week, giving him four more days having to wear what he'd begun to think of as his 'butler mask.' As much as he became excited at the idea of leaving, he'd have liked his employers to be a little less jaded by the whole thing.

"You'll be back," Bob Cohen said. He was in such a foul mood when Ricky brought his coffee to him that Ricky had an inkling the foursome hadn't gone so well. Ricky had been forbidden from telling anybody which TV show he was going to be on. He was happy to keep his mouth shut. He was beginning to worry about being a gigolo on a show called *Bought and Sold.*

Ricky kept a smile on his face as he topped up Bob's coffee several minutes later.

"So, what's this TV show you're on?" Bob asked.

"Sorry, I can't say."

"Huh. You certainly are the mysterious one. You've got everybody talking." He slid his business card across the small table toward Ricky. "Don't forget your old friends when you hit the big time, bus boy."

Ricky took the card, to be polite. He was no bus boy, not that there was shame in an honest day's work, but Bob wanted to wound him and yet he was asking Ricky for a favor. *Include me.*

They weren't old friends. Bob was an ass. He walked back into the kitchen and tossed the card into the trash. He washed his hands thoroughly because he had no idea where that card had been.

The thought occurred to him that he was very squeamish about illicit sex for a guy who was about to play a gigolo on TV.

Later that afternoon, he called Stephen, who told him that until the contracts had been signed he would hear nothing more about the show.

"This is the tough part kid. This is where you sit and wait."

Two days went by, during which he plagued Stephen with constant calls, and his roommates with his incessant fears. Had he quit his job too soon? Stephen had said they'd start shooting next week. He wanted to get ready for the part.

"So, get ready," Max insisted. And so Ricky went and got his first facial, panicking when the esthetician squeezed a pimple on his chin he never even knew had been there. She promised him the redness and mild swelling would go down by the following day.

But it didn't. The pimple grew bigger. It mocked him. He was so unglued at this point that Max dotted some toothpaste on it before Ricky went to bed, promising him it would make the pimple vanish by morning. He awoke every hour between midnight and seven a.m. checking the pimple. It looked a lot better, which was encouraging. He'd never had a blemish in his life, not even as a teenager. Why did he have to start now, on the eve of his sparkling new career?

Everyone he met, even customers, gave him pimple advice. It was embarrassing.

He thought the damned thing had finally given up the ghost, and he went to work with confidence on his last morning at Jerry's. He had a surprise visitor . . . Drake. Ricky felt the weird tug of attraction mingled with fear as soon as he saw the man. Drake held him with his gaze. It was as though he reached right into Ricky and grabbed him by the solar plexus and just . . . squeezed.

Drake sat in a booth large enough for six people. Ordinarily a lone customer would have been given a smaller table or directed toward the counter stools. Ricky guessed that Drake hadn't waited for the hostess to escort him to a table. He also figured nobody had had the balls to tell the man to move.

"They told me you were always early for your shifts," Drake said. "Please, take a seat."

"I . . ." Ricky wasn't supposed to hobnob, but he was off the clock and this was, after all, his last day.

"What in the world is going on with your chin?" Drake asked.

Mortified, Ricky clapped his hand to it. "Nothing."

"You have a pimple. It'll clear up by the time we start shooting." Drake gave him a lazy smile. "So you gave notice, and this is your last day."

Ricky nodded, suddenly wishing he had a cup of coffee. He needed to do something with his hands.

"You have integrity. I guessed that about you." Drake finally let go of Ricky's eyes. Ricky hadn't been able to look anywhere else during this whole exchange. "Most people would have just walked out." Drake seemed to be waiting for a response.

Ricky shrugged and, oddly, it seemed to hurt, as though he were pulling his body out of ice. "Um. No. I couldn't do that. I need to have a place to come back to. You know, in case things don't work out."

Drake looked surprised. "You think the show won't work?"

"I don't know. A lot smarter guys than me have waged bets on great shows that didn't work."

"Such as?"

"Moonlight." *Oh, man. Could I sound any dorkier? Vampires? But oh, boy I loved that show.*

"The one about the woman who turns her husband into a vampire on their wedding night?"

Ricky nodded.

"I liked that show, too. Pain is love. Do you believe that?"

Ricky wasn't quite sure what that was supposed to mean. He thought about how hurt Shellene had been when he'd told her he couldn't marry her. "I think love is a pain," he responded.

"That's not quite the same thing. You don't like pain?"

"Of course not. Does anyone?"

"Depends on the pain." Drake gave him a long look. "And, of course, who's inflicting it."

Ricky didn't know what to say to that. *Pain is love,* Drake had said. What was he doing here anyway? He couldn't have come to see Ricky. *Oh, no.* For one brief moment Ricky panicked that maybe Drake was another prospective sleeping partner for Bob and his wife.

"I came to see you even though I shouldn't," Drake said, surprising him.

This guy is spooky. Can he read my mind?

"You shouldn't? Why?"

"Protocol. It's how things are done. We hide behind our attorneys and agents until all the i's are dotted, and all the t's are crossed."

His smile so disarmed Ricky that he could only stare into those fathomless brown eyes.

"Your agent tells me you have your heart set on moving into the house on Stradella."

Ricky came back to earth with a thud. "Yes, I do. I love that house, even from the photos."

"It's magnificent. You have great taste. I've made sure you can have it. It will be in your contract, of course." Drake hesitated and for the first time seemed a little uncertain. "In that house you'll have complete privacy. When we bring cameras in there it will be with your advance knowledge." Again, the man paused. "Are you going to live there alone? I mean, do you have a boyfriend?"

Ricky was surprised by the question. "I'm bringing my two roommates. They're a couple. I don't have a boyfriend." They locked eyes again. "There won't be much to film there. Sorry." For the first time, Ricky felt annoyed. He'd begun to realize how intrusive all this would be. He was going to be a gigolo but already he could tell the lines between reality and fiction would be blurred. What if he had a client he really liked and the big fat cameras were there? What about Max and Colin? Would their privacy be invaded? Did Colin, a rising name on the tennis circuit want to be filmed living with a gigolo?

And, holy moly. How could he stop Pa from ever finding out about this show? Why hadn't he thought about this before?

He reached into his pocket, his fingers on the hunt for his lucky silver dog. He resisted the urge to repeat in his brain, *there is no place like home.*

"Not having a boyfriend is probably easier," Drake went on. "Boyfriends don't always understand when you have to date for a living." He leaned back in his seat. "I run a gay escort service in Las Vegas and it's been very successful. All of the gigolos on our show will technically operate out of Vegas, where prostitution is legal, but you will all be living in LA to service rich men here."

Pa doesn't watch cable. And I know they're officially going to call me Marcel on the show. Stephen said it's sexier. God. What the hell have I got myself into?

Aware of Drake's gaze on his face, Ricky nodded. He hated the word prostitution, but it was the reality behind the flippant-sounding *gigolo.*

"Your first date will be next week. You'll be handling a

client who likes to frequent sex clubs. He specifically wants you. I know you're an actor, but I want you to be okay with this."

"That's nice of you." Wow. Ricky wondered if all the gigolos would be getting visits like this. He couldn't help feeling that there was something Drake was holding back. He was about to ask when his shift manager came to the table.

"Sorry, Ricky. We're getting busy and Bob Cohen's about to have a cow."

"I'll take care of him. Sorry, Joe."

"No problem." The manager raced off, a thousand other little fires clearly needing to be put out.

Drake put his hand on Ricky's arm. "I don't want you to worry about anything," he said.

"I'm not worried." He blew out a sigh. "Much."

Drake grinned. "Of course you're worried. But I'm gonna make you a star, Ricky." He shook his head. "I mean, Marcel. I think you're the guy everyone's gonna be talking about. I just want you to know I will look after you. I won't let anyone hurt you."

Ricky found himself once again tongue-tied. He thanked Drake and went off to take Bob Cohen's order, even though he knew the man would never deviate from his usual litany of complaints. Or his poached egg and whole wheat toast.

Two days later, the contracts had been signed and Ricky received the keys to the house on Stradella. Stephen. Max and Colin accompanied him to view it. Colin had Googled the address and they'd all been agog at the details. Driving up the sharp incline to the world-of-its-own Bel Air was one thing. Seeing the house, situated on an entire acre, in person, was something else. Built in 1931, the sprawling, seven-thousand foot Spanish-style ranch house dripped opulence. It was gorgeous.

The surrounding gardens were lush and the colors of the bougainvillea and myriad of tropical flowers almost blinded Ricky with their richness. When he'd seen the folder full of photos on his audition, he'd been taken by the image of the drop dead gorgeous pool and matching cabana house that was a mini replica of the main house.

Seeing it up close, he knew he'd made the right decision to select the five-bedroom, seven-bathroom estate that had recently been sold for eleven million dollars. Eleven million! He couldn't wrap his head around figures like that.

And he could barely take in the genteel splendor of the beautifully restored home with its original dark wood floors, high ceilings, beams, and its views of Hollywood. He'd never seen anything like it.

Max and Colin were speechless.

"And you really want to us to move in with you?" Max asked for the hundredth time.

"Of course I do. Which bedroom do you want?"

"You choose first. My God. Look at the outdoor eating area. Think of the dinner parties we can throw!" Max threw his arms around Ricky and hugged him. "I love this place. And I love you!"

Ricky chose the bedroom overlooking the pool. He'd always wanted . . . no, longed for . . . fantasized about having a built-in pool. The bedroom was magnificent. He loved everything, including the massive walk-in closet. At home he'd had a portable clothes rack for as long as he remembered. The bathroom resembled something out of a hotel catalogue. The sunken tub had whirlpool jets and two showers. He'd never seen *that* before.

He could hear Max and Colin running through the house with Stephen, laughing and having fun. Ricky sat on the bed, his fingers rubbing the little ears of the silver dog in his pocket. He rubbed until the pads almost hurt.

Pain is love.

Ricky started to cry. The house was beautiful. Everything was beautiful. He felt so grief-stricken though, thinking of all the people he knew back home who lived in ramshackle places. Old Man Wilson, whose house had been declared unfit for human dwelling. Ricky and Pa had tried to help him fix the place up, but the local council ordered the property to be condemned. Old Man Wilson wouldn't take help beyond what Pa and Ricky had done and shot himself in his barn.

He thought of all the people in Bourbon who could fit in here quite comfortably.

And then he felt some pressure on the bed beside him.

Colin.

"You okay?" Colin slid his arm around him.

"Yes. No." Ricky swiped at his tears with the back of his hand. "I can't believe I'm here."

"You deserve it, Ricky. You've worked hard. Never forget that. All those double shifts, the pain-in-the-ass customers."

"Pa worked hard all his life, too."

"He used to beat you."

The words hovered between them. Shadows and fog.

Pain is love.

He couldn't deny it. He would never have told Max and Colin had he not had night terrors the first few weeks he'd been living with them. The horrors of what Pa had done to him had receded to the past. Or so he'd thought.

One night, his panic attack during his sleep finally brought the couple to his room. Pa had hit him for everything. If he had a bad day on the farm, if he lost money on his favorite horse, Ricky suffered the consequences.

"He gave you a bloody key ring when you came out here. You needed cash. You had seventeen dollars in your pocket," Colin said now. He tightened his hold on Ricky.

Ricky allowed his friend to hug him. It strengthened him. He had to remember he'd had a dream and followed it. Max and Colin had encouraged him to tell him their fears. The night terrors stopped. He didn't think he had them anymore.

When they left the bedroom and he saw the one his friends had chosen he had a momentary qualm. They were so far away from him. He'd feel so alone in his room. However, they seemed ecstatic over their room that had French doors leading to a balcony with a small table for two. Very romantic. Very Max and Colin. They, too, had a walk-in closet and fancy bathroom.

"Ace Andrews really wanted this place. I heard he even fucked Drake Hardy to try and persuade him to give it to him," Stephen said. For some reason this really bothered Ricky.

"Which house did he end up getting?" he asked.

"The one Bing Crosby used to own in Beverly Hills."

The estate on North Beverly Drive would have been Ricky's second choice. He wondered what Ace Andrews would do to the property and imagined one giant orgy constantly taking place.

"I'm most interested to find out what happens when Cliff Becker moves into his digs on Stone Canyon." Stephen's evil smile was unsettling.

"Why's that?" Ricky asked.

"Well, he's a Raëlist."

"A realist?" Ricky scrunched his nose. Weren't most people?

"A Raëlist. It's a religious cult."

"It is?" Max and Ricky asked in unison.

"What do they believe in?" Colin asked.

"They believe they're alien beings. They believe in cloning. They claim one of their followers gave birth to a cloned human. Oh, and they practice sensual massage." Stephen clearly enjoyed holding their attention. "They say they wish they'd cloned Adolph Hitler."

"What?" Ricky exploded.

"Relax. They want to bring him to trial and make him pay for his crimes."

"I think I like this cult," Ricky said.

Stephen nodded. "They're as wacky as hell, but their hearts are in the right places. They say the aliens will come down here and make all the guilty pay for their crimes."

Ricky hadn't been told who the other gigolos would be. He tried to recall which one Cliff Becker had been. Later that afternoon, he and Stephen attended a private screening of the extended trailer for the series that would begin to play on the Elysium network that night. They sat in one of the conference rooms in the company's Santa Monica headquarters as, one by one, the other gigolos arrived. Ace Andrews arrived with a man who wasn't particularly handsome, but turned out to be an Italian businessman. They'd been together ten years and Luca was not only Ace's life partner, but managed his career and booked his private escort appointments.

He seemed very nice and talked about their recent ski vacation in the Swiss Alps. Ricky wondered how Luca could bear to see his lover with other men.

Cliff Becker was a handsome enough guy. His brown hair had been cut in a military style. He looked like the bossy sort. A hot-looking African American man captured everyone's attention. He exuded authority and sensuality at the same time. Trevor, a former Special Forces and had just completed his third tour of duty in Iraq. He shook hands with each and every gigolo.

"Thank you for what you did for our country," Ricky told him, shaking his hand.

"It was my pleasure." Trevor lifted Ricky's hand to his lips and kissed it.

Boy, he was a sexy one.

The final member of the group strolled in. Ricky recognized him as a gay model who'd been part of the No8 campaign. Now that Proposition 8 was no longer an issue in California and same-sex marriage had been legalized, he wondered what the guy was up to.

His name, according to the introductions made was Rick. That was why Ricky had been forced to live with Marcel. It irked Ricky to discover that Rick was Stephen's third client. Why had he fought for Rick to keep his name and not Ricky?

A kind of shimmer ran through the room as the door opened and Drake walked in looking impeccable in a silvery grey suit with a V-neck white T-shirt. He caught Ricky's glance and smiled. That didn't go unnoticed. Not that Ricky minded. As he greeted everyone, they all clustered around the slightly dusty boardroom table. The lights dimmed and a big-screen monitor came down over the wall closest to the door. Chairs and heads swiveled as the peppy music came on first, followed by the visuals.

Ricky was stunned to hear Blondie singing 'Call Me.' This had been the music theme for *American Gigolo*. As the credits zoomed across the screen, footage shot from the party and the one-on-one interviews played. Ricky's heart pounded in his chest as he watched himself identified as Marcel.

The producers had cut his interview and pieced it together to make him sound like a mystery man. A country boy at heart but put up with the bright lights of Hollywood because he was searching for that one man who would make him happy.

God almighty. *How did they manage to make me sound like a complete fool?*

Ace sounded like a cock-hungry whore. Especially when he said he wanted to die in bed surrounded by hot young men and he wanted to have three cocks in his mouth as he took his last breath.

Rick turned out to be a former hustler who'd worked for a

brothel in Las Vegas and had fallen in love with a john. "I call it my *Pretty Woman* moment," Rick said in his interview.

Now he was back and anxious to meet lots and lots of men.

Cliff, the cultist, came off like a complete lunatic. Especially when he said he had asked his Raëlist superiors if it were possible to clone James Dean and bring him back to life so Cliff could give him a sensual massage.

"The aliens are monitoring our behavior. Everything is going into their computers and then will come judgment day."

Okay, then. Clearly the aliens either turned a blind eye to sex for money, or they believed in more than sensual massages.

The one who came off worst though was poor Trevor, who sounded like a nine-year-old girl. The former war vet said, "I just want my clients to love me. Isn't that what we all want? To be loved?"

Ricky was shocked at how the footage had been cut together to make it look like the five guys were friends. Apart from one hello to one another at the party, Ricky and Ace hadn't said more than two words together but somehow looked like they were the best of friends. A lot of footage had been used from the party, but also from their auditions and the final one-on-ones.

The final images showed all five men walking down hallways. Separate but together. The last shot was Ace knocking on a hotel room door and swiping a key card, just about to open the door.

Bought and Sold a caption read across the screen, the words looking like a stamp.

There was silence for a moment. The lights came back up and everybody spoke at once.

"You're hot," Ace said across the table to Ricky.

"Thanks. So are you."

Luca and Ace gave him friendly smiles. The others all grumbled about their appearances. Ricky was more worried about what they hadn't seen. What would happen whenever they entered a hotel room.

Thank God he'd have a full crew with him whenever he entertained a client.

While everyone talked, Drake spoke over them, silencing them all once again.

"We're going to have some special training in cotillion for you."

"What's cotillion?" Rick asked.

"Are you joking?" Trevor snapped. "French ballroom dancing?"

Once again, the group chatter reached an instant crescendo. Drake silenced them all with one hand, waving a finger in the air.

"Not only ballroom dancing. You'll be taught the art of conversation, fine dining, manners, and"—he gave a dramatic pause—"then we'll go clothes shopping."

"I don't want to learn that shit," Rick suddenly shouted over the top of the other voices.

"Suit yourself. If you want to look like an asshole eating from your knife the way you did the other night, it's on you," Ace responded.

"No." Drake looked each of the five new gigolos in the eye. "It's in your contract. You do as I say."

Ricky didn't care so much about learning a few manners. He cared that he hadn't really read the contract. He'd trusted Stephen with the details and had been more worried about sending Pa some money every month. Stephen had arranged for four hundred dollars to be funneled from his paycheck every month directly into Pa's savings account.

For Ricky and his father, it was a lot of money. As time

went on, Ricky wanted to send him more, but for now, it was a hefty chuck after Stephen and the tax department took their share of his income.

Seconds later, Lisa Lee, a famous Hollywood stylist, a stick-thin blonde who had her own TV show, arrived. Armed with a film crew on one side and a coterie of assistants on the other, she bore armfuls of clothing swatches that seemed to weigh more than she did.

In a weird moment, she and Ace pulled down their underpants and compared butt tattoos. Ricky wished he could scrub his eyeballs as well as his brain. He'd never seen an anorexic woman's ass before.

In a crossover promotion, Lisa's show would feature her helping the stars of *Bought and Sold* prepare for the cameras. *Bought and Sold,* in turn, would credit her as the resident stylist. She'd evidently been studying all five men because she and two on-camera assistants, a scared looking man and a frantic, Nicorette-chewing girl, began fussing over the gigolos.

Two limousines took the five men to a banquet hall in Pasadena where Drake was already waiting for them. They had to sit at round dining tables and practice drinking water from champagne, martini and lowball glasses.

"Sip. Don't chug," Drake advised. "If you're uncertain about which knife or fork to use, remember to start from the outside and work your way in toward your plate."

The staff at the banquet hall brought them each a plate of food.

"Never eat a bite of fish with any other food, in case there's a bone in it," Drake continued. "I'm going to show you how to eat correctly, and how to deal with bones. You are about to enjoy a rainbow trout and they have lots of bones."

He joined them at the table. Lisa Lee kept drinking water.

Ricky wondered when she'd last had a decent meal, then observed her eating a pea.

A single pea.

Ricky watched Drake deftly and elegantly debone his fish without making too much of a fuss. He also showed them the correct way to squeeze a lemon over their food so that it didn't spray across the table and into other people's eyes.

Oddly, the only one who had perfect table manners was Ace.

"Sweetheart, I've lived and worked all over the world. Nobody would pay to screw me if I had the eating habits of an ape," he said when Ricky complimented him.

Trevor and Rick had particular trouble with their lemons. They kept rolling under the table. The two men spent a long time underneath the tablecloth. Ricky began to wonder if they were really hunting for lemons, or were they falling in love?

Next, they danced.

Ricky both feared and longed to dance with Drake, who didn't come near him. Drake and two other men from the production staff danced with them all. Ricky was disappointed that Drake didn't dance with him, even when they tried the flouncy, ballroom thing. Trevor excelled at that.

Next, they were taught some basic dance moves that were close to dirty dancing. Ricky loved to dance and enjoyed the hip swiveling he did with Ace. He kept watching the way Drake performed with the others and wished he could grind against him.

Some of the banquet room staff looked aghast at the men dancing together but said nothing. Music filtered out from a tinkly sound system that lent an air of unreality to the whole thing.

This beats waiting on tables. That's for damned sure.

The afternoon flashed by in a whirl of light and laughter. And then came the shopping. Lisa took the gigolos to a private men's show room at Neiman Marcus in Beverly Hills, where racks of clothing awaited them all.

It impressed Ricky tremendously to see how well organized this scene of inspired chaos really was. In the few minutes Lisa spent directly with Ricky he fell passionately in love with her fragrance and the way she visualized him. She'd picked out an array of 'essentials' as she called them, from the Tom Ford collection. Sweaters, shirts, pants, shoes, even sunglasses. He looked at himself in the mirror.

He was no longer Ricky Marcel, Beverly Hills waiter.

He was Marcel. A new gigolo in town, who looked like he already knew his way around it. He liked how his body responded to the cut and clarity of the two suits she'd picked out for him. She'd even selected underpants and socks, and kissed his cheek, gently shoving him out the door to have his hair trimmed.

"They want you to grow it out, but they kind of want the angel look. A halo of curls," the petrified male assistant said as he escorted Ricky down the street to something called the Juan Juan salon. The assistant's stomach rumbled so loudly Ricky could hear it.

"You need to eat," he said, frowning.

"I'm not allowed to eat. It's in my contract," the poor guy shrieked.

Ricky shoved him into an Italian bakery. The two inhaled appreciatively. Ah. bread. Oh, joy. Cheese.

"She'll kill me," the shivering man whispered.

"Blame me. I'm the evil doer. Come on, split a sandwich with me." Ricky pointed to a blackboard menu.

The assistant, whose name turned out to be Todd, chose a cheese and warm salami sandwich. Seconds later, Ace and his lover, Luca arrived.

"Jesus, I'm famished," Ace shouted. "I ate a plateful of bones for lunch!"

Ricky wondered how Luca had found them and realized for all his sexual bravado, Ace was very attached to the guy. It made Ricky like Ace all the more.

"I'll have what they're having." Ace jerked his thumb toward Ricky and Todd, who kept looking over his shoulder in a panic-stricken way.

When the sandwiches arrived, even Ace stopped talking as they ate hastily.

"You know," Luca said midway through his sandwich half, "I don't think I ever tasted anything better in my life."

"I think I'm having an orgasm," Todd whispered. "I want to make love to this warm salami."

The others laughed. Ricky wanted to pay, but Luca picked up the tab. Ace gave him a swift kiss on the lips before running off down the street with Ricky and Todd.

"My headache's gone," Todd said when they entered the salon. "My God. I actually feel quite good!"

He doted on Ace and Ricky as they got their hair makeovers. Ricky got a careful trim that took no length from the back or sides, but added layers, and a few highlights around his face.

By the time he was done, he looked in the mirror, hardly able to recognize himself even though he hadn't had a lot of work done to his hair. He stared at the wisps of curls the hairdresser had formulated as if by magic. He seemed lit from within, the highlights in his hair making his eyes glow.

Wow. And now I guess it's show time.

Later that evening, he showered in his new house and got dressed in a pair of new rust-colored leather pants that were buttery soft and made him feel very sexy. He put on a cool short-sleeve black Tom Ford top that had a zippered neckline, pairing this ensemble with black boots. He ran to Max and Colin's room. They were almost ready.

"Look at you, hottie." Max grinned at him.

Ricky was grateful his best friends in this crazy city could join him. He and the other five gigolos were supposed to go on a bar hop. At this point, Ricky felt very comfortable with Ace and Luca, but was still uncertain about the other gigolos. Cliff seemed nice, too, but his constant, dire warnings about alien interventions creeped Ricky out a little.

Max drove them all to Santa Monica Boulevard and to the Revolver, the first gay bar where they were supposed to meet. Drake had insisted that they visit a few bars and, later, a restaurant, with the show's crew in tow. They would shoot additional footage to use in *Bought and Sold's* opening credits and for future episodes. In the meantime, they were fast-tracking the whole bonding thing.

Ricky noticed all the gigolos had brought their posses. Each gigolo looked completely different, except for Trevor who looked like he had the same haircut and wore the same outfit he'd had on earlier that day.

Ace wore low-slung jeans that didn't even cover his ass crack, and a tight red jacket that didn't close and came just below his nipples. Only he could pull off such a wacky, fuck-me outfit.

Cliff wore sunglasses because, he told them, the aliens couldn't see him then. The film crew for the show arrived and the house manager, Jeffrey, offered them all drinks. Trevor ordered a Maker's Mark and smacked his lips that it hadn't been watered down.

Jeffrey looked affronted at the mere suggestion. The five gigolos were strategically placed around the bar, their assorted friends and loved ones pushed out of camera range but decorating the bar as well.

Ricky had been here many times with Max and Colin and some of his other friends. It was weird however to be in here without music pumping out of the place. The TV show's producers had arranged for a half-hour's quiet time with early patrons signing off as background characters.

Cliff ordered a martini; Ace, a Dos Equis with a whisky chaser; and Rick pompously ordered a cognac.

Ricky ordered his usual Cosmopolitan, even though he didn't really like it. He just remembered Carrie Bradshaw used to drink them on *Sex and the City* and for some strange reason it was the first drink that came to mind whenever he had to order.

"You are so gay," Ace teased.

Ricky laughed. The guys bantered a bit, then Ace looked to his left and asked Cliff to explain why the aliens couldn't see him behind his sunglasses. Cliff gave an incoherent explanation that had the others working hard not to laugh. He was a good sport about their ribbing. Ricky guessed that was the price one paid for belonging to a weirdo religious cult.

Aware of the cameras, Ricky relaxed under Ace's gentle control. He poked fun at everybody, even himself.

At one point he leaned closer to Ricky and said, "You're going to get guys sending you drinks. Don't fucking touch anything you haven't seen poured."

This was old advice for sure. Ricky had always heard that if he left his drink to dance or use the john, to abandon the drink when he returned. The urgency in Ace's tone worried him. Suddenly, two fresh Cosmos arrived in front of him, but when he looked around, Max and Colin were waving to him.

Clowns.

He waved back, grinning at them.

"Now, pretend your friends didn't send you these. You know how to act like you're drinking something so you don't hurt your fans' feelings?"

Ricky stared at him. "No, I don't think I do."

"I'll show you." Ace grabbed one of Ricky's drinks and

leaned across the bar to grab a couple of short black straws from a caddy that featured maraschino cherries, sliced limes and lemons. "These are perfect. Look, just put it in and sip, but see how I'm holding it? I'm squeezing it halfway up the straw to prevent any liquid actually touching my lips. As soon as you can, release some of it."

"Where?"

"Anywhere but in your mouth. Last think you need is some weasel slipping you a roofie. And when you can, give the drink to the bartender."

Ricky began to feel uncomfortable. Ace instructed him constantly on what to expect and not expect.

"Don't carry a wallet. I keep my money in my shoes, or Luca carries it for me."

After about forty minutes at The Revolver, Drake arrived, looking terrifying and sexy in a black suit and dark purple shirt with a matching tie.

"There's something about him," Ace said, catching Ricky's glance in Drake's direction. "I didn't take you for a sub."

A sub? Ricky knew what that meant and began to feel really stupid. Now he understood Drake's comments about pain being love. Goddamit. Drake was a Dom.

"You know what they say about Doms, right?" Drake asked.

"No. What?" Ricky tried to tamp down the dismay he felt.

"They all started out as somebody's boy and they're looking for their Dom again."

Ace slugged back Ricky's drink. "Fucked if I know what's in this, but I like it." He raised his glass toward Luca. "I need to go check up on my mine." He swaggered away and Ricky was left alone. He moved toward his roommates, but Drake waylaid him.

"I've arranged your first date for tonight."

"What?" Ricky wasn't ready. He wanted to bolt. He wanted to run. He felt for his lucky key ring but it stuck out in his leather pants so he'd left it at home.

"Are you ready?" Drake asked.

"Not really. I thought we were supposed to bond."

"You've done plenty of that. I've already told your roommates that you're going to be home late." He put his hand to Ricky's back, steering him out of the club. Outside, a sleek back car awaited them. Several guys tried to talk to Drake, but he pushed right past them. He held the back door of the vehicle open for Ricky, who felt as though he'd just been consumed by a huge spider and wasn't sure he wanted out of the web.

Ace had told him Drake was a Dom. Maybe he was, maybe he wasn't.

"What can you tell me about my client?" he asked as the driver, whom Ricky could barely see, peeled slowly away from the curb.

"I'm the client," Drake said, and his mouth came down over Ricky's.

Chapter Four

Ricky gave in to the all-consuming kiss, shocked at how much he wanted it. He couldn't believe how alluring a kiss could be. Damn. Drake knew what he was doing. Ricky grew dizzy, hungry for the other man's mouth.

Drake pulled back suddenly, grinning. "Been a while for you, has it?"

Ricky nodded, staring at Drake's mouth. He wanted to do more kissing.

"You're a great kisser. Better than Ace."

Ricky's mental haze lifted. "You kissed him?"

"Sure. Why not? I wanted to see what the fuss was."

"Did you have sex with him?"

Drake stared at him, glancing at the driver. "No." He said the word in a tone that suggested not yet.

"Will you kiss all the guys?" Ricky asked.

"No." That was more emphatic. "I'm attracted to you, Ricky. Can't we just leave it at that for now?"

Ricky nodded. He'd always had a terrible habit of wearing his heart on his sleeve with men he liked. And then he'd have to work hard covering up his passion in front of other people. Drake seemed to withdraw from him. Jimmy would do that, too, when he was alive.

Why had Jimmy gone to Iraq and died? Sometimes, back home, when things had gotten really bad with Pa, he'd gone to Jimmy's grave in Fort Scott and talked to him. Once, he'd thrown himself on the ground, sobbing, wishing desperately that the grass would open up and swallow him whole. Jimmy had taken Ricky with him when he died. He'd taken Ricky's soul. He'd taken the sunshine with him.

How were you supposed to live when love was taken from you? How were you supposed to pretend there wasn't this big, gaping hole in your body where your heart used to be?

He sank back against the leather seat. He had begun to feel better once he'd made the decision to leave Bourbon. His heart had healed. He felt less like dying, less like wishing Jimmy had never gone to war and they'd run away out west together to follow their fortunes like they'd planned. He blamed himself for not being able to leave Pa, for feeling guilty about the old man's poor health.

The reality was, he'd worried about the animals in their lives. When their lost dog up and died, he saw it as his sign it was time.

Just like Jimmy secretly up and joined the Marines, Ricky bought a one-way Greyhound ticket to Hollywood.

Pa had gone mad, but by then, Ricky longed to escape and left him a note. He'd gone to hide out over his last few days with the only friend who didn't fear Pa's wrath . . . Jimmy's older brother, Woody.

But Pa had tracked him down and promised to see him off at the bus station, telling him that Ricky had been a good son, and he would give him 'a little something' to help him with his new life.

A key ring.

Damn, that had been a low blow.

Pain is love. Ricky thought he understood those words now. Pain had filled him. Fueled him. Fed him. Pain had kept him alive. Feeling.

Drake must have lost somebody he loved, too.

"I'm sorry." Drake's hand covered his. "I like you, Ricky."

Ricky stiffened. "Don't you mean Marcel?"

"Ricky. Marcel is your stage name. I did that to protect you. Marcel can help you go places. You can choose to tell your family what you're doing. Or not."

"Pa might not watch cable, but one way or another, he'll find out." Ricky said the words aloud.

"You're afraid of him."

Ricky shrugged. "Not as much as I used to be. I got away."

"Ah. I had an abusive father, too. You won't find me abusive, Ricky. I'm just trying to make this work for both of us."

Ricky was confused. Why was Drake his first date?

"Where are the cameras?" he suddenly asked.

"They'll be there, but I wanted some time alone with you first. I had an idea." Drake paused and Ricky looked up into the other man's eyes. He saw empathy and pain there.

"I would like to be your exclusive date." Drake gave him an embarrassed smile. "I don't think I can bear to see another man touch you. Not after I've watched you butter a bagel."

"Excuse me?"

"I watched you prepare breakfast for that idiot man at Jerry's. You buttered his bagel with such care. You even apologized to the bagel when you dropped it face down on the floor. The man was a total prick to you. You could have gotten your revenge by still giving it to him. Instead, you apologized to the bagel and threw it out and toasted another. That's integrity. That's heart. You even took the man's crap when he whined about how long you'd taken. I want to protect you from idiots like that. I was wrong to cast you. You're too sweet for this work."

"Are you firing me?"

"Of course not. You're going to be huge. You're going to be the shining bright star in our show's sky. But if I'm going to be your exclusive date, I hope you're going to be okay with some of my sexual preferences."

"You're a Dom." Ricky began to worry about what all of this meant. Would Drake be cruel and mean? Would he stick pins into him? He'd seen a horrible DVD with needle play. It had been awful watching the long, thin instruments piercing a grown man's muscular arm. The man had sobbed as wooden clothespins had then been stuck to his nipples and abs.

"Who told you that?"

"Ace."

Drake sighed. "Ace has a big mouth. That's why he and I will never play together."

"Did I just get him into trouble?"

"No. But the fact that you're still sitting here is encouraging. You're not running down Sunset screaming for the hills."

"The car's moving too fast. Wait until we get to the next red light."

Drake laughed. It was the first actual laugh Ricky had heard from the man. It was like a river running over rocks. Ricky loved the sound. Drake leaned forward and said to the driver, "Run all the red lights."

The driver laughed, and so did Ricky. In the bad section of Sunset, past the cute boutiques and outdoor cafes, the car rolled to a stop against the curb. The driver got out and held Ricky's door open. He slid out, Drake quickly next to him on the sidewalk. A vagrant approached them and Drake spoke to the man with quiet dignity.

Ricky was surprised to see him hand the guy a one hundred dollar bill.

"There you go, my brother. You have someplace to stay, tonight?"

The man shuffled his feet against the ground. It broke Ricky's heart to see that the shoes, if one could call them that, had disintegrated and had been clumsily repaired with paper and tin foil.

"I've got friends." The vagrant's voice came out in a deep burr. Ricky glanced at his neck. There was a huge growth hanging off it.

"If we take you to a place where you can get a hot meal and a bed for the night, will you accept it?"

The vagrant kept brushing his feet against the ground as though he couldn't stand still.

"I'm okay," he said, and limped away.

"That was nice of you," Ricky told him.

"You might find it hard to believe, but I am a nice guy."

"Really?" Ricky deadpanned.

Drake shook his head, but he didn't seem angry. "You're a mouthy one, for such a pretty boy." He gazed down the street as the vagrant turned a corner and vanished. "He used to be a world champion boxer. I heard he fell on hard times but I had no idea he was this bad." He turned to his driver.

"Smithy, call Jake and ask him to come get Gordy Fuller."

"The vagrant?" The driver looked mortified.

"He needs our help. Please ask him to take Gordy to our friend Alex. He'll help him get a room for the night. Tomorrow, I want his neck looked at. Tell Alex I'll take care of the medical expenses."

The driver nodded.

"Call me when you're back."

"Yes, sir."

With his hand on the small of Ricky's back, Drake steered him down a dark, narrow alleyway.

"Wait for us, please, Smithy," he said over his shoulder to the driver.

Where the hell was he taking Ricky?

Ricky felt a little claustrophobic as they squeezed between two decrepit-looking buildings and suddenly he could hear a burst of music coming from the right. A red door. A strange series of knocks and a tall man opened it.

"Good evening, Mr. Hardy." The man held the door wider.

"This is my friend, Marcel."

"Good evening, Marcel."

"Marcel, meet Mr. Walsh."

"Nice to meet you, Mr. Walsh." They shook hands, Drake's arm still around Ricky as he seemed to deliberate between two closed black doors.

He turned right and they plunged into a cold darkness, the door closing behind them. Ricky could still hear music pumping from somewhere. Blue fog enveloped them.

"Relax. It's a harmless mood enhancer," Drake told him.

Dang. Drake seemed to read him so easily. "What's in it?" Ricky asked as his eyes adjusted to the faint light.

"Lavender oil, chamomile, S-Adenosyl-Methionine. All natural stuff." Drake pressed his free hand to the wall and an opening emerged. They passed through it, into a room with blue and yellow lights tinkling from tiny tree branches like millions of fairies from the ceiling.

Ricky looked up in wonderment. He'd never seen anything like this. The hardwood floors beneath his feet reflected the lights around him. He heard soft moans, then the sound of slapping. A woman in a maid's outfit was bent over a gym horse and another woman gave her a solid beating against her red and bruised-looking buttocks. Men and women dressed in maid outfits swirled around them, the music pumping louder now.

"What would you like to drink?" Drake said into Ricky's ear. "And don't tell me a Cosmopolitan. I could tell you don't like those."

"How could you tell?" Ricky had to shout above the fray.

"I was watching you." Drake took his cell phone out of

his pocket. He slid his finger across the screen and showed the image to Ricky. The other gigolos were dancing at The Revolver.

"How–"

"I have cameras everywhere," he said.

"Even here?"

"Even here." Drake gave him a quick kiss. "What would you like to drink? And I mean like."

"I love gin and tonic."

Drake seemed surprised. "Your roommates told me that, but I didn't believe them."

"Why not?"

Drake shrugged. "I felt sure you'd be more the champagne and caviar type."

What in the world made him think that? Ricky shook his head. "I'm like Lucy Ricardo. I'm more the beer and pretzel type."

When Drake laughed, Ricky felt happy.

What else did they tell you?" Ricky tried hard not to stare at a woman sitting on the floor, her shoulders bleeding as a man in a black leather mask stuck feathers into her skin.

"Feather piercings are the latest thing," Drake told Ricky. "Your roommates told me a lot. They love you."

"I love them."

They pushed through the section where people were getting needles in their backs, chests and arms. It unsettled him. One naked woman lay on the floor apparently in a mixture of pleasure and pain as her Dom applied electricity to her genitals. She had a variety of needles in both thighs.

She's a human pincushion.

Memories of Pa driving a nail into his foot when he caught Ricky putting nail polish on his toes bit him hard. He took a deep breath. He'd been ten and already feared his attraction to Barbie dolls and other sparkly things. He and Jimmy had bought Holiday Barbies for each other online from the first Christmas they'd been together. Ricky had hunkered for a vintage Malibu Barbie with tan lines and Jimmy had given it to him. They'd hidden their 'girly gifts' in Jimmy's mother's basement. She'd been a love. She'd left her house and, when she died of untreated breast cancer, Jimmy and Woody inherited the property.

Woody had made it clear that Ricky was family and was welcome any time. He, too, was gay, but knowing what their nasty little town was like, he had a lover in Kansas City and spent all his weekends there, away from prying eyes.

He'd offered Ricky a refuge from Pa's savage beatings, but Ricky feared Pa's retribution. Now, as he looked around at the people flogging, whipping, torturing one another, he saw only pleasure and controlled pain.

"In this universe, nobody is here unless they want to be," Drake told him.

Ricky saw a couple walk by in head-to-toe yellow latex. Small slits over their eyes didn't show much of their eyes. Yellow ball gags in their mouths startled him.

"They're into water play," Drake told him.

Ah. Yellow for the color of pee. He'd seen men peeing into one another's mouths in gay porn, but it did nothing for him.

He saw a naked, bald woman sitting on a sofa crying. Every instinct in him made him want to run to her and hug her, but another woman soon sat next to her.

"Don't worry," Drake said. "She's upset because they won't pour hot wax on her head."

"She wants ... what?" Ricky had heard of such things. Well, he'd glimpsed it in some porn movies, but that didn't float his boat either.

"Sometimes players don't know when they've had enough. She wants pain for all the wrong reasons. We protect people from themselves when that happens."

Ricky was fascinated by this. There were some actual rules and safety standards in this community. He liked that.

"Do you like the idea of exclusivity between us?" Drake asked him.

"I do." *If it keeps me from having this stuff happening to me, sure.*

"Would you be willing to wear a cock cage for me?"

Ricky stared at him. He'd been asked this question during his very first interview with Jessica. Man, that seemed so long ago now.

"I don't think I know what it is," he said truthfully.

"I suspected that when I saw your audition." Drake gave him a disarming smile. "I suppose you think it has something to do with chickens."

"Yeah. To be honest, I did."

Drake laughed. "I love your honesty. Come on."

He started to lead him away but Ricky was struck by a woman on her knees on the floor, her face and body bound in what looked like plastic wrap. The only things left uncovered were her back, nose, and scalp.

A man stood beside her with a blowtorch in one hand, a huge red candle in the other. The candle dripped wax all over her.

"The higher you hold a candle away from a body, the less it hurts," Drake told Ricky.

"I never knew that."

Drake smiled. "I have so much I want to share with you."

It was on the tip of his tongue to ask, *why me?* but he didn't. He allowed Drake to lead him to another room, where they were alone.

"Are we being watched?" he asked Drake.

"At the moment, yes."

"Cameras are where?"

"The window to your right."

Ricky looked but could see nothing. It was dark and looked empty. He took in the bed that had been made with crisp white sheets and a black duvet. A tray stood beside the bed with their drinks. Drake took him in his arms and kissed him. When his right hand moved down to squeeze Ricky's ass, Ricky moaned into Drake's mouth, his cock springing to life against the other man's thigh.

"Good," Drake murmured, letting his hand brush against Ricky's boner.

Their kiss went on. Ricky loved the fragrance of the man. He couldn't quite identify it. A mixture of things. If he'd been asked to describe Jimmy's smell it would have been Drum tobacco and cotton candy bubble gum. Even now, seeing either in a store unglued him.

Drake had a different smell. When he broke off their kiss and began to lick and kiss Drake's throat, Ricky saw surprise flare in the man's eyes.

Ricky couldn't stop his attraction to this man showing itself in the way he touched and kissed Drake.

This time, Drake didn't stop him. He didn't push him back as though he were an over-eager puppy. He took all the desire and the swampy, dark lust Ricky had harbored, kept dormant. He took it and gave it back to him, unzipping Ricky's top. He took it off, their hungry mouths meeting before the top was even over his head.

Ricky caught a glimpse of fire out of the corner of his eye. He wanted to look, but couldn't. He was so worried this would stop. That Drake wouldn't want him.

He had to touch him. Angels were on the balcony of his mental room somewhere because when he slid Drake's jacket from his shoulders, he could feel the contained heat of the man's body. He liked the silkiness of the shirt and the hard muscles beneath it.

"I lost my lover, too," Drake said against his lips."

Ricky went crazy then and almost ripped Drake's shirt off.

"Easy, easy. Just undo them one at a time," he rasped as Ricky almost tore off a button. "I'm not going anywhere."

Ricky almost wept. Jimmy went away. The had loved each other, and their fucking, even their lovemaking, was always quick. They had to be quick. They took their sensual moments where they could.

This was a whole new world to him. Drake took his time, making sure Ricky was comfortable. He stripped Ricky naked, stroking his cock with an assured hand. He wouldn't let Ricky finish undressing him, however.

He backed Ricky over to the bedside table with their tray of drinks. He held a lowball glass to Ricky's mouth. Just that afternoon, Ricky had been taught the correct way to drink a cocktail, but right now, he couldn't for the life of him remember how to do it. He gulped, but Drake didn't seem to mind.

"Let me taste," he said, his tongue darting into Ricky's mouth.

He put the drink back down and pushed Ricky gently to the bed. Kneeling before him, Ricky couldn't believe it when he raised his head and looked down to see Drake licking his toes.

That was new. And, surprisingly, it was alluring.

He watched the way Drake licked and sucked his way up Ricky's legs. By the time his tongue touched Ricky's ball sac, it was all over. Ricky came with a shout. Drake grinned up at him.

"I had a feeling that might happen." He began licking at Ricky's juices, his tongue sliding across Ricky's belly and down his groin. Ricky groaned as Drake held his legs apart and began licking and sucking his ass. Ricky wanted the man's tongue inside him forever.

Drake pulled something out of his pocket.

"What is it?" Ricky wasn't afraid, just curious. He stared at the large gold ring.

"A cock ring. Ever used one before?"

Ricky shook his head.

"I want you to last a little longer this time." Drake went back to work sucking Ricky, and then moved up his perineum to his balls. He gently licked and bit the sac, making Ricky gasp with pleasure. Drake coaxed his joy with extra kisses and licks, then snapped the gold ring around Ricky's cock and balls. It was tight but not painful.

Ricky's ass involuntarily came off the bed as Drake held his hips and began sucking on his cock. It had been so long since he'd had a blow job and nobody but nobody had ever taken their time with him like this, savoring every ridge and every inch of his shaft this way. Ricky knew he had a good, long cock. Jimmy always said so, but Drake seemed to really appreciate it, too.

Drake sucked him all the way into his mouth. Ricky could feel his cock sinking into moist velvet and gave a cry as a tremendous orgasm ripped through him.

When Drake released the cock ring, a fresh tremor rocked Ricky's body. Drake stayed on him, swallowing everything Ricky had to offer.

When he'd stopped coming and the fire receded in his brain, Ricky said, "That was amazing."

Drake smiled and got up. "I'm going to ask you to wear this cock cage for me."

Ricky leaned up on his elbows and watched Drake produce a strange-looking clear cock-shaped container that came in two parts. Drake put on the first part, which sat snugly around his balls, his cock dangling from it.

"This is a chastity belt. You will be able to pee but you won't be able to masturbate. If you get very uncomfortable, call me and I'll come and remove it. I would like you to keep it on until our next date, but I will remove it if you can't stand it."

"You mean this is it?" Ricky couldn't help feeling bereft.

"For now."

"When is our next date?"

Drake smiled. "You're eager."

"I am."

"How about breakfast?"

Ricky nodded eagerly. "Sounds perfect." He let Drake pull him to his feet and looked down as Drake put the rest of the cock cage onto him and locked it shut.

"You belong to me now," Drake said, and kissed him.

He slowly re-dressed Ricky and led him out of the room. Ricky almost begged to stay but saw a man tied to some kind of wheel being flogged by a burning whip.

The man wielding the whip worked up an amazing rhythm and Ricky held his breath as each sting landed on the prone man, the flames forming the shape of a heart.

"Fire flogging," Drake told him.

"You like to do that?"

"Not really. I prefer other things." Drake led him outside into the cold night air.

"Such as?"

"Kinbaku." When Ricky wrinkled his nose trying to figure out what that meant, Drake said, "It's Japanese rope tying. Very sensual and artistic. Some people call it Shibari but it's really Kinbaku."

Whatever he called it, the prospect frightened Ricky a little, even though it intrigued him.

"It requires trust and I hope one day I have yours." Drake stepped forward and kissed him. "Call me and tell me you got home okay? How do you feel?"

"I feel like I don't want to leave you."

Drake kissed him again. "I mean, how is the cage?"

"All right. Weird. You're sure I can pee wearing this thing."

"Absolutely. You just can't jack off or fuck."

Ricky nodded. The cock cage was already unpleasant. It was gonna be a long night. Drake's car rolled up and he held the door open, making sure Ricky got inside. He sat back against the seat, trying to get comfortable. It wasn't easy in his tight pants. He longed to undo the zipper to have more room, but whatever he did, the cage chaffed him. He couldn't call Drake right now and tell him he wanted it off. No. He wanted to be with Drake. He didn't want to be a wuss and have the man pick another gigolo to make his own.

He tried to distract himself with the view of Sunset late at night. He suddenly saw a woman walking down the street, sandals in her hand.

"Stop!" he shouted to the driver.

The driver jumped, but did as he was told. Taking a deep breath to stave off the stab of pain in his groin as he moved too quickly to open the door, he ran out onto the sidewalk. He knew this woman. It was Bob Cohen's wife. He didn't know her first name, but called out. "Mrs. Cohen!"

She stopped in her tracks and turned. Her eye makeup had turned into a river of years and she threw herself into Ricky's arms.

"What happened?" he asked her.

She just sobbed hysterically. He instructed the driver to keep going as they got back into the car. He took her home with him.

Max and Colin were thankfully back and fussed over her as Ricky changed his pants. His cell phone rang. He was pleased to see it was Drake. He took the call, pleasure igniting his whole system.

"Who is the woman?" Drake asked.

Ricky explained.

"My sweet boy." Drake's voice turned soft. "Call me before you go to bed, okay?"

"I will."

"How's my cock feeling?"

"It misses you."

"I miss it, too." Drake ended their call and Ricky raced into the kitchen where Mrs. Cohen sat, her fingers around a mug of tea, and told them how her husband had hired a hooker for them a couple of weeks before. She'd hated it and he'd promised her his cheating days were over, but she'd just caught him in a cheap motel on the strip.

"My marriage is over," she said.

The three men let her talk. She spent the night in one of the guest rooms and Ricky went to bed, staring out at his view. He wanted Drake to be with him.

He wanted love.

He didn't want to be a gigolo. He would lose everything, he knew that, but he couldn't do this. He was already getting attached to Drake.

Damn. I signed a contract.

He didn't call Drake. He was too busy agonizing over where he could run, how he could hide. He heard a car and then heard the alarm go off in the house.

An exchange of words in the hallway.

Shit. It was him.

Ricky stiffened in the bed as his door opened and he knew, just by the smell of his skin, that it was Drake.

"You were supposed to call."

Ricky stared ahead. He couldn't look at him. "I don't know if I can do this."

"Would you like me to remove the cage?" Drake came and sat beside him. He was a mixture of tender and harsh. His special smell was lime soap and melons. That was how he smelled.

"Yes. No." Ricky turned to him, looking up at Drake's beautiful face in the moonlight.

"There's going to be consequences for disobeying my orders."

Ricky nodded. He wondered what that would entail.

"We need a safe word. Is there one you prefer?"

Ricky looked at him. "A safe word?"

"For whenever you think things are too much. Such as the cock cage."

"Oh."

"You pick the word." Drake looked at him.

Ricky felt helpless. He was stepping deeper and deeper into a world that both terrified and intrigued him.

"How about Lucy?"

"Lucy?"

"She's my favorite comedienne. She got me through a crappy childhood."

Drake grinned. "You constantly surprise me." He stepped forward and kissed him. When they broke apart, both breathing heavily, Ricky asked,

"Who was the lover you lost?"

"John Dragon. He was my master for fifteen years. He died in a car accident three years ago. I don't think he got over my desire not to be his slave anymore. I loved him, but I needed some space. He got drunk and drove. Bad combination."

Wow. Just like Jimmy. They got mad and got themselves all torn up.

"I'm sorry."

"Me, too." Drake lay beside him.

Ricky leaned into him, Drake spooning him.

For a long moment they lay there. He became aware of Drake's even breathing. Man, he was asleep!

Ricky slept on and off. He'd never actually spent the whole night in bed with a man. He liked it. As morning came, he turned over to look at Drake's perfect face, but he was gone.

Wow. Just like that.

He called him, but it went to voice mail. He left a second message, then a third. Where the hell was he?

Ricky took a shower, feeling disgruntled and abandoned. Did they even have a breakfast date?

He got dressed in board shorts and watched his roommates frolicking in the pool.

"You're grumpy," Colin observed, getting of the water and sitting beside him on a chaise.

"Drake spent the night, then vanished."

"I saw him in the kitchen. Mrs. Cohen was having a meltdown. He called his driver and took her back to her car on Sunset."

Ricky sighed. "That was nice of him."

"In spite of everything, paying off her black granite Amex card is the most important thing in her life," Max said, hoisting himself out of the pool.

"My cock hurts," Ricky suddenly said. It didn't really hurt, but he'd begun to whip himself up into a state of panic over the cock cage. Drake had told him to call him and he had. And Drake hadn't responded.

"What did he do to your cock?" Colin looked wide-eyed.

"Put it in a cock cage."

The two men burst into laughter. "I adore those things," Max said.

"You do?" Ricky was stunned.

"I make him wear one all the time." He pointed to Colin, who nodded.

"Show me the cage," Colin said. His friends crouched around him as he pulled open the Velcro fly.

"That's a training one. You'll be fine," Colin said. "Have you called him?"

"Three times."

"Maybe he's punishing you," Max said. "Did you misbehave?"

"Did he give you a safe word?" Colin asked.

Safe word. Shit. He'd forgotten about that. He stumbled back to his bedroom and called a fourth time. He made sure he said Lucy a few times. As he peed in the bathroom, the door opened.

Drake.

Ricky stared at him.

Drake grabbed him. "I was waiting for you to use the safe word. And don't forget I told you there'd be consequences for disobeying me."

But he saw how distraught Ricky was and soon stopped talking and began kissing him. He unlocked Ricky's cage and left it on the vanity.

"I'm giving you a short break from it. But it goes right back on, okay?"

Ricky nodded. He'd started to feel naked without that thing on. In a weird way it made him feel as though Drake were always with him, squeezing him, as if to say, *I am here. I am with you.*

"Are we on camera?" Ricky whispered.

"Not yet." Drake covered his face with kisses, shoved Ricky's board shorts off completely and got himself naked in record time. His body was beautiful. Ricky loved the way Drake kissed and held him, then put him on the vanity.

He kept his gaze glued to Drake's enormous cock and knew he would spend hours and hours pleasuring him.

Drake bit off a condom foil and gloved up.

His gaze locked with Ricky's. They didn't speak for a moment, yet Ricky knew they both had a lot to say.

"I want to love you, Ricky. I want to be with you. I don't

want any other man to touch you. Can you live with that?"

"Yes, please."

"Fuck." Drake grabbed his face and kissed him. He rubbed his cock against Ricky's legs. Ricky opened his thighs and grabbed Drake's ass.

"I'm . . . I'm already there. I already love you. I don't want to lose you. But I'm afraid of pain. I'm afraid of death," Ricky rambled.

"I won't make you do anything you don't want to do." Drake kissed him and knelt between Ricky's thighs. Before he could start licking Ricky though, Ricky stopped him.

"No, don't. I want you to fuck me. I'm ready. I need this."

Drake lost no time rubbing his cock against Ricky's hole. It was all new and different and just amazing. He loved the sensation of Drake pushing his way into him. He glimpsed fire again out of the corner of his eye and realized it was them. Their heat.

He was just a gigolo for the cameras, but for Drake, he was something else. He could feel it. The electricity crackling between them. Drake's cock drilling into him was the best thing that had ever happened to him.

"I feel it, too," Drake said against his mouth and fucked him hard and deep.

Ricky tried to hold onto him with legs and arms but his body had a mind of its own. He flailed and wailed as he got royally fucked. They came together.

They collapsed against one another and Ricky smiled when Drake said, "I'm going to fuck you in the bedroom for the cameras this time. I think I'm gonna have to tie you to the bed."

"I'm not going anywhere," Ricky said, wrapping his legs around Drake.

Drake carried him to the bedroom. Ricky had no idea how the other gigolos were going to react to him being the exclusive date of their show's executive producer, but if he had his way, Drake wouldn't even think about looking at another guy. And one day, he'd make Drake wear a cage, too.

Hadn't Ace said he was a Dom in search of a master? Weren't they all?

He gave up all thoughts of anything but pleasuring Drake, who dropped him to the bed with a gentle thud. They melted into one another's bodies.

Ricky loved the sounds they made when they were with each other. And he loved their mingled smell. Sex. Passion. Melon. Lime soap. Laughter. And hope.

Chapter Five

Early the next morning, Colin, Max, and Ricky began moving their belongings from the old place and into Stradella when the marshals arrived to post the notice of foreclosure proceedings on the door. Colin oohed and aahed over their sexiness. Ricky fretted that he had to be at Drake's house for the first group meeting for the show.

"Go," Max said. "We'll take care of it." He kissed Ricky's cheek. As Ricky ran to his car he saw the shocked looks on the marshals' faces. Men kissing one another! Oh, the horror.

He drove all the way into the Hollywood Hills, already anxious to see Drake, and, truth be told, the other gigolos. It was the first morning in months he hadn't awoken to the prospect of dealing with grumpy customers and his constant nightmare that he would somehow screw up his orders. The stress was no longer there. He had a TV show!

Roaring up Beachwood Canyon was quick and easy this time. No traffic jams, no valets. He'd taken care to put on his sexiest outfit. He was getting used to looking like a pirate. He parked across the street from Drake's house, careful to observe the convoluted parking signs. Ricky had been caught more than once in his early days here in LA. He hated getting parking tickets.

At Drake's door, the man himself opened it, looking pale and drawn.

"Is everything okay?" he asked Drake.

Drake nodded. "One of our gigolos wants off the show."

That was a shock. "Which one?"

"Trevor."

"Has he told you why?"

Drake led Ricky inside with a brief kiss on his lips. "I swear, part of the reason I didn't want to hire actors, I mean working actors, is that they're such pains in the ass. Now this guy gives all the divas I ever met a run for their money."

"What does he want?" he asked Drake.

"I don't know, sweetheart. Maybe you can talk to him. I've got to get Cliff out of my vegetable patch. He's convinced the asparagus are tiny baby aliens with secret messages for him."

Okay, then. Ricky hustled into the living room and found Trevor sitting on the sofa with a remote control in his hand. He was watching CNN and the news was never good. Trevor needed to find something happy to watch.

"Hey," Ricky said, as he approached.

Trevor looked up.

"Can I join you?"

"Free country." Trevor scowled, as though these words might be faulty.

Ricky sat on the sofa, but not too close. Trevor was in a strange mood. Pa used to get this way whenever something didn't go right. In Pa's life, that was a lot.

"What's going on?" he asked Trevor.

"Nothing. I'm trying to tell our fantastic producer I want off the show. He's waving the damned contract in my face like it's ironclad. Shit. I wish I'd gotten into the French Foreign Legion like I wanted. I do *not* want to be here."

Ricky had never met anyone who'd tried to get into the French Foreign Legion. He thought that only happened in movies.

"They rejected me," Trevor said. "They said I didn't have what it takes to disappear. They said I'm confused."

"Are you?"

Trevor glanced at him in surprise. "I'm bisexual," he said. "When I'm with men, I want to be with women. When I'm with women, I want to be with men." He looked at Ricky as though expecting him to be shocked.

"Which do you prefer?"

"Apples and oranges," Trevor said. "How can I choose?"

"Who says you have to?"

Trevor opened and closed his mouth. He stared at Ricky, narrowing his eyes. "You trying to be funny?"

"No." Ricky shrugged. "I don't see your problem."

"My problem is I'm on a show about gay gigolos. Now all I can think about is women."

Ricky grinned. "Still don't see your problem. Women are going to love you. Half the planet is full of them. Maybe you'll get all the couples and you can fuck both the men and the women."

Trevor looked at him. "Yeah. I hadn't thought about that."

"I think it's cool you like both. I wouldn't want to be with a woman, but that's just me."

"What about Ace?" Trevor asked. "Think he'd do a woman?"

Ricky leaned back into the sofa, a little more comfortable now. "I don't know. I can't imagine Ace liking anything that doesn't have a cock."

A burst of laughter startled them both. It was Ace. He threw himself between Trevor and Ricky and kissed them both.

Drake walked into the room, his eyes as hard as pebbles as he saw Ace draped all over Ricky.

Ricky tried pushing Ace off him, but Ace was fooling around now, rubbing Ricky's crotch, then Trevor's.

Trevor laughed a deep guttural laugh that set the others off. "Boss," he said finally, "Country boy got me thinking.

I'm gonna stay."

"Good," Drake said, but he didn't look very happy. He turned on his heel and left the room.

"He doesn't like me messing with his stuff," Ace whispered in Ricky's ear. "I hope he doesn't punish you for this."

Oh, boy. Ricky didn't like the sound of that. He knew what punishment felt like and didn't look forward to it.

As the other guys arrived, Ricky felt the weight of Drake's gaze on his face. A woman Ricky recognized from the party walked into the room bearing a huge tray. She unloaded pots of tea and coffee, plates of pastries and bagels onto a large, glass dining table by the double glass doors that led onto a small balcony.

She gave them all a smile.

"Hello, Ana." Ace strolled over to her and kissed her cheek. She blushed under his attention. He put his arm around her. "No matter what anyone says, you're the woman of my dreams."

She rolled her eyes this time and left the room.

"Women!" Ace pretended to huff, and reached for a bagel.

When Ana returned with eggs and a massive piece of smoked salmon, the guys raided the table. A camera crew appeared and, suddenly, everybody was on their wackiest behavior as the sound girl began popping microphone packs onto everyone's trousers. Cliff held an asparagus stalk, stroking and whispering to it.

Drake caught Ricky's eye finally and smiled.

The ache in Ricky's gut subsided.

As they filled their plates and poured their coffee, Drake opened the doors to the balcony. The strong odor of skunk invaded their senses. It made Ricky's eyes water. They all raced back inside again, but the smell had followed them.

"Come in, little Sheba," Cliff kept saying to the asparagus.

Trevor tore it from his fingers and ate it.

"Shut up, little Sheba. Tasty little Sheba," he said, making Ace laugh.

"You just ate the mother ship." Cliff looked aghast.

"My God. I think it's beeping inside me." Trevor clutched his stomach in a dramatic way, his eyes widening. "It's saying something."

"What? What's it saying?" Cliff tried to put his ear to Trevor's belly.

Trevor backed away. "It's saying . . . wait. It's saying . . . you're an asshole."

Cliff straightened. "I think you're making fun of me."

"Ya think?" Trevor rolled his eyes, grabbed the guy's head and kissed him. "Good thing I like crazy."

"I'm not crazy."

"Yes, you are," everyone chorused.

Cliff looked wounded. "I won't forget this when the aliens get here," he said.

"I'll take my chances," Rick muttered.

Ricky watched all this going on, aware that the cameras were filming everything. It was a beautiful day in Hollywood. The house, the view, even the goofy banter were the kind of things he'd envied back home in Bourbon. He'd watched *Queer as Folk* on Jimmy's TV and dreamed of being an actor out here.

The others must have had their own ambitions. He knew he'd get to know his co-stars and already liked them. He gravitated toward Ace more than the others, and Ace seemed to favor Ricky, too.

"Luca and I want to take you to dinner," he said, cornering Ricky at one point. "Off camera, of course. If you want to bring Drake, it's cool. By the way, whatever's goin' on between you two, he seems damned happy."

Ricky's cheeks flamed. Happy? Drake seemed surly and

pissed at him today.

The camera crew found Ricky and Ace by the bathroom door and Ricky shot inside to get away from them. A few seconds later, Drake knocked at the door.

"Let me in," he said. It was a command, not a plea.

Ricky opened the door.

"You kept the mike on. We can hear everything. When you need to have a private conversation or a quick pee, turn it off."

Ricky felt the blush returning to his cheeks. "I'm so sorry, Drake."

"Don't be sorry. You did a fantastic job with Trevor. That little scene will look great on our first episode." He turned Ricky around. "I'm going to turn it off." He reached into the back of Ricky's pants and turned off the switch. "I am going to have to punish you, though."

Ricky took a deep breath. "How?"

"I'm thinking a spanking might be in order." He kissed Ricky and fondled his ass. He watched Ricky unzip his fly and take a leak and seemed to take delight in dressing him again. "I'm thinking you might need to wear the cock cage again."

"Okay." Ricky wondered what the spanking would be like. He didn't want to displease Drake in any way. He did, however, hope that some rocking sex would go along with the spanking.

Back in the living room, Rick told everyone about his first date, which had taken place early that morning on Santa Monica beach. "This guy wanted me to do tai chi with him, then he wanted me to have sex in his SUV right in the parking lot."

"And?" Trevor asked.

"And, he's married. On the down-low. I was giving him head when his wife called asking what was taking so long.

And I thought, 'Man, I'm working as fast as I can!'"

The others laughed.

"So many guys are on the down-low," Drake said. He flashed a glance at Ricky. "In my past experiences, I found the married guys especially appreciative. For most of them, we're their first male lovers and they cherish us. I got some of the best gifts from those clients."

"Funny you should mention that." Rick pushed back his shirtsleeve and held up his right arm. "Look at this. It arrived here by messenger an hour after I left the guy."

Trevor squinted across the table. "Is that a real Rolex?"

"It better be, soldier. I'd been admiring this online and mentioned it to my client. It's a reconditioned, vintage 18-karat yellow gold President day date watch. It's got a gold fluted bezel, and a champagne tapestry stick dial. Have you ever seen anything so gorgeous?"

"I don't know. How much was it?" Ace asked.

"Ten grand."

"Then I've never seen anything more gorgeous in my life." Ace put his feet on Trevor's lap, ignoring the withering looks from the other man.

Ricky sat back in his chair and watched Drake talk to the others. He tried not to think about the spanking. His cell phone vibrated in his pocket. He thought he'd turned it off. He checked the readout the second Drake took a call and the camera crew took a break.

It was Max, letting him know their move was complete.

As the group broke up for the day, only Ricky stayed in the house. For about an hour, he waited alone on the sofa. He had the remote, but didn't feel like watching TV. He was sorry now that he hadn't actually eaten anything earlier, but he'd been too nervous. He tried to think about what he'd be doing in his previous existence. He checked the time on his cell phone. He'd be gearing up for the lunch crowd at

Jerry's.

He couldn't help smiling at the thought that he'd come a long way in just a few days. Aware of Drake's presence in the room, he looked up. The gravitational pull was so alluring and yet, still so unsettling to Ricky, who wanted to bounce from the sofa and throw himself into Drake's arms.

They grinned at each other. "Ever been to the Inn of the Seventh Ray?" Drake asked.

Ricky shook his head. "No. I haven't. It sounds like something Cliff made up."

Drake laughed. "Not quite. But I'm sure he'd like it. I'm taking you there to dinner. Until then, I want you naked and in my bed."

Ricky got to his feet and almost cantered as he followed Drake to his bedroom.

It was really something. Heavy silk curtains gave a boudoir feel to the space. Not to mention the bed with its posts and artistic surroundings. Ricky noticed a bed tray laden with a tea pot, cups, and . . . a pair of gloves. On second thought, the gloves weren't a pair. One was dark green and black leather. The other seemed to be made of something soft and cuddly.

Oh, boy. Ricky swallowed hard. He was in for it now. That he knew.

"Take your clothes off," Drake commanded.

Ricky did as he was told. He wondered if Drake would give him expensive toys during the duration of their relationship. Actually, he didn't care. He stood naked before Drake, who seemed to drink in Ricky's appearance. He didn't remove a stitch of his own clothing.

"On the bed," he said, his tone low and husky.

Ricky moved to the lavish-looking bed, afraid of messing it up, but Drake stood beside him, throwing back the covers. As soon as Ricky's fingers connected with the satin sheets, he thought he'd died and gone to heaven. Drake sat beside him on the bed.

"I'd ask you to lay on your belly, but I see your cock is very hard." Drake seemed happy, and that made Ricky happy. "Would you like some tea, Marcel?"

Ricky's eyes widened. He knew now they were on camera. He wondered where the crew was, but soon didn't care.

"The tea you're about to enjoy is an aphrodisiac tea." Drake stared at Ricky's cock but didn't touch it. His gaze was so full of longing, Ricky felt his erection grow even harder.

Drake let out a sigh.

"What's in the tea?" Ricky asked.

Drake licked his lips. "Um. Ah." He frowned. "Black galingale. It's a Thai infusion created specifically for men." He reached across Ricky and poured out a cup. Ricky liked the small curls of steam drifting out of the pot. He sure wished Pa would never see this. He wished they had complete privacy, but damn it, he had a horrible little show-off inside him who gulped up all the attention. He leaned up on one elbow as Drake held the cup to his lips.

He drank, even though the tea was hot. It was good, too. It tasted like nuts. He touched his tongue to the roof of his mouth, aware of Drake's feverish stare. After he finished sipping, Drake put the cup back on the tray, poured himself some and drank it all down.

"The more you drink this tea, the more you will find your orgasms become very intense," Drake said.

Ricky didn't respond. He was so afraid he'd come again and tried to focus on something sad. He had plenty of those things in his memories, but Drake leaned down and kissed him right on the chest. It was such an intimate place to kiss him that Ricky inhaled sharply. He felt great. Relaxed and sexy, ready for anything. As he watched Drake slide the leather glove on his right hand, then the furry one on the left, he almost amended his thoughts.

Drake pushed Ricky back to the bed, stroking him with the furry hand. Ah, cashmere. He liked the way the silken weave felt against his skin. Drake sat beside him, his gestures assured and enticing. He put his hand between Ricky's legs, letting the cashmere drift over Ricky's ass and balls, finally letting it run up the length of Ricky's shaft. Suddenly, the leather glove came into Ricky's eye line, and he watched Drake rub it over his body. When the glove came to Ricky's left nipple, Drake took his time making circles. Ricky thought he might drown in pleasure.

Hastily, Drake rolled Ricky over. With his cock squashed beneath him, he felt his ass rising off the bed of its own accord and the first stinging slap connected with his butt cheek. It didn't hurt. Far from it.

Drake alternated between stroking with cashmere and spanking with leather. Soon, the leather glove came down on his ass repeatedly and he squirmed in a myriad of sensations. The slaps were like nothing he'd ever experienced. They seemed to ignite fires deeply extinguished within him. He started to come, but Drake stopped him by squeezing the base of his cock.

He flipped over a panting Ricky and held the right index finger of his gloved hand to Ricky's mouth.

Ricky sucked. Drake gave him a second finger to suck. The gloved fingers were big, but turned him on. Drake took them away again. He softly spanked Ricky's inner thighs to get him to open his legs. Ricky opened them, stunned when Drake turned him over and spanked him harder, flipping him back once more. Again he gave his gloved fingers to Ricky to suck and began rubbing them against Ricky's asshole. Ricky thought he would die if they didn't get inside him soon.

Using the cashmere glove, Drake stroked Ricky's leaking cock with one hand and slowly fucked him with the leathery fingers on the other hand. Ricky felt the fabric slide inside him, soft and hard all at the same time. Drake kept up a maddening pace, and Ricky was unable to breathe as the tension that had been building in his ass took hold of him. He came hard, all over the cashmere glove, his ass cheeks clutching at the fucking fingers inside him.

Drake couldn't stand it anymore. He ripped off his clothes, produced a rubber and speared Ricky with the biggest, thickest cock Ricky had ever seen. His ass hurt from the spanking and from the leather glove but his orgasm did not abate. He grabbed Drake to him, the two of them enjoying his wild ride.

When Drake came inside him, he grinned down at Ricky, who gazed up at him.

"Wow, Drake. I was never a size queen until now!"

Drake laughed. "Glad to hear it. Did you like getting spanked?"

"Hell, yeah." He loved the feel of Drake's hard, golden body atop his. "How much of this will wind up on the show?" he whispered.

Drake smiled down at him. "A little. You were fantastic, my little country boy."

Ricky forgot about everything else except being in his lover's arms. Drake started all over again, stroking, kissing, licking him, long after the camera crew had gone home and the tea turned ice cold. He didn't even mind when Drake put the cock cage back on him.

"How long were you a hooker?" he asked Drake.

"A few years. I had a totally crap pimp. I realized I could serve men better by taking care of both my sex workers and my clients." He got dressed and glanced at Ricky. "Do you want to have dinner with Ace and Luca, or will you let me have you to myself?"

Ricky loved having the choice. "I'd like to be alone with you, or will that get me more punishment?"

Drake laughed. "No more punishment tonight, baby. Your ass is on fire."

Ricky didn't mind. "I kinda like how it feels. I think I could keep coming."

"As soon as I get you home, you will," Drake promised.

Ricky liked the sound of that. He liked everything that was happening. He didn't mind when Ace sounded so disappointed about not seeing them for dinner that he and Drake changed their minds.

"Can we invite Max and Colin, too?" Ricky asked, snuggling against his lover in the backseat of the limo.

"Of course we should invite them." Drake didn't hesitate to call Ricky's best friends. As Smithy drove them to pick up the other two couples, Ricky felt bigger than life. Bigger than anything he could have expected in his career as an actor. He was afraid to pinch himself, in case it was all a dream. But he knew he wasn't.

He was more than just a gigolo.

ABOUT THE AUTHOR

A.J. Llewellyn lives in California, but dreams of living in Hawaii. Frequent trips to all the islands, bags of Kona coffee in her fridge and a healthy collection of Hawaiian records keep this writer refueled. A.J. loves male/male erotica, has a passion for all animals—especially the dog, the cat and the turtle. A.J. believes that love is a song best sung out loud.

To find out more about A. J., visit www.ajllewellyn.com or you can email her at AJ@AJLlewellyn.com.